Destined
—Or—
DOOMED?

Destined
—Or—
DOOMED?

KIERRA SMITH

DESTINED OR DOOMED?

iUniverse books may be ordered through booksellers or by contacting:

iUniverse
1663 Liberty Drive
Bloomington, IN 47403
www.iuniverse.com
1-800-Authors (1-800-288-4677)

ISBN: 978-1-4917-5255-5 (sc)
ISBN: 978-1-4917-5256-2 (e)

Library of Congress Control Number: 2014920723

Printed in the United States of America.

iUniverse rev. date: 11/20/2014

Acknowledgments

I'd like to thank God for gifting me with such an amazing talent and for blessing me with people who appreciate and accept my style of writing. The support has been amazingly unbelievable and I am humble as well as thankful.

This book is dedicated to our troops and war heros; I'd personally like to thank:

My Cousins: Daryl Snipes, Jr., Kevin Brown, Kevin Tate – Brown and Terrell Brown.
My Uncle: Jerome McBride
My deceased Uncles: Anthony Brown and Marvin Roper
My deceased Grandfather: John L. Brown
Family Friend: Jerral Harrison

For your bravery and your perseverance to uplift and protect this country, we salute you!

I hope my readers enjoy every page!! I continue to write because of you!!!! Don't forget to post your feedback on Amazon and Barnes & Noble!

Check out the books that are coming next, they are located at the back of the book!

"Lucky is the man
Who is the first love of a woman,
But luckier is the woman
Who is the last love of a man..."
Author Unknown

Prologue

With her body arching at the touch of his slender, but strong fingers, he claimed presence down her body. Igniting flames in every spot that he touched, leaving behind the residue of ashes as she burned.

As much as she wanted him to hurry because she couldn't take anymore, it seemed as if he were moving in slow motion. He bit her neck as he deliriously traveled towards her ear and slipped his tongue in its opening. Pulling the flesh between his pearly white and impeccably straight teeth, he elicited a moan from her closed lips.

Intertwining his hands with hers, he allowed her arousal to be expressed through the digging of her hands into his skin. He knew what she needed, but he also understood it would take time to give it to her.

He found her lips in the midst of the storm that was brewing, while escalating the awaiting ecstasy. She dragged her freshly manicured nails up and down his spine, causing him to falter in his pursuit.

She trapped his waist in between her thighs as her hands fumbled with the waistband of his pants to free his erection.

She didn't know what to expect, but it wasn't the package that was delivered. It was just as chocolate as the rest of his body and appealed with the same manner as his chiseled shoulders and thick, yet defined six packs that were plastered into her.

Swiping his lips over her ear, "You ready?" He breathed.

Feeling as though her air supply has been temporarily suspended, she nodded with a lump in her throat.

"If you need me to stop, just say it. I know I'm a little bigger than you expected." He caressed her lips sensually while slowly sucking on them. Sending a shiver down her spine and residing along the flesh that enveloped her hips.

With one hand, he balanced his body weight so that he wouldn't add any additional pressure on her. Using the other hand, he guided his penis into the entrance of her frontal lobes, but paused at the resistance. With his eyes boring into hers, he added more pressure onto her center.

Her tightness caused him to inhale and hold his breath. Tightening her hold, she closed her eyes as he pushed a little harder to enter her body. Once the piece of skin subsided for further entry, he succumbed to the whiff of lightheadedness and moaned. "Baby."

"I know." She paused, "I feel it too!" She couldn't help but moan with him in response.

He slid out of her swollen lips and re-entered, making her gasp for air after his mouth crashed down onto hers. She bit down to communicate the new-found desire that was stirring deep within her walls.

She found a rhythm with him as they began to rise and fall to give each other the ultimate satisfaction of an orgasm. He knew that she had never experienced it before and his stamina was slipping with every stroke. But, he was determined to be her first in every area.

With his length, he pushed her passed her limits. The sensation started in her feet and traveled up her legs and settled in the pit of her stomach. His stroke increased with every moan that escaped her lips, signaling a silent plea not to stop.

He grabbed her hips and executed a thrust that sent them both off the cliff where ecstasy soon awaited.

Emotional and vulnerable, she prayed that she would never have to give him up because she couldn't and after tonight, she wouldn't.

Waking from her re-occurring dream Myah was panting and out of breath. As she looked over at the sleeping body in her bed, she was thankful that she hadn't awakened him. Something had to give because she couldn't possibly entertain one man, while the other continued to torment her every night when she closed her eyes to sleep.

Chapter 1

S itting on the edge of her chair, Myah Johnson couldn't help but glance at the door every time she felt a presence go by. Continuously, she scolded herself for calling even though she would have regretted not notifying him. She wasn't well-versed with the regulations and protocol of the United States Army, but she knew that she had to get him here and fast. If Myah was certain of anything, the repercussions of an uninformed Lance were bound to erupt a volcano.

Myah looked across the room at the lifeless body lying in the hospital bed. It had been four days and her older brother Micah was still in a coma. Feelings of desperation and vulnerability were beginning to set in because they were running out of options and she was trying to hold on. Her parents had resorted to praying and fasting for Micah's full recovery. Trying not to lose faith, Myah said a silent prayer, placing her forehead in the palms of her hands.

But in the midst of the prayer, her body tensed and the hair on the back of her neck stood up. It was undeniable that someone had entered the room. No one had to tell Myah who it was. She felt him before her nostrils could process his smell. It was the way her body stood at attention as he silently commanded every fiber of her being to obey him. Dreadfully lifting her head, she paused to stare into the eyes of her brother's life-long best-friend. Myah hated to

1

stare directly into them because it seemed as if they pierced through her like a racing bullet. Despite the strain of space and distance after six years nothing had changed.

Myah's heart skipped several beats as she tried to clear the lump lodged in her throat. The ringing in her ears cut off the signal in her brain that told her mouth to speak. Walking further into the room, Lance knew he should have looked towards the bed where his friend since the age of five laid, but Myah held his gaze.

He could see the distress on her face, but it didn't wrinkle the beauty she possessed that he had always admired. Myah had a soft caramel glow with sharp Chinese eyes and high cheek bones with a few freckles that hid in the shadows. She was simply a china doll that had come to life. Unsure of who should speak first, he did, "Hey love, how are you holding up?"

She smirked at his words of endearment because the reality was that she had always loved him, Myah couldn't remember a time when she hadn't. At the age of eight she had created and envisioned her life with Lance who was sixteen years old at the time. But at the ripe age of twenty-five, Myah concluded that her fantasy wasn't destined to become a reality.

Rising from the chair, she met Lance at the center of the room and wrapped her arms around his thick yet soft frame. Relishing in the firm but not quite rough hug that he offered, Myah surveyed the Army fatigue that gracefully fit every inch of his large body structure. Lance was a giant at 6'2" compared to her 5'4" frame. "I'm glad you were able to come so quickly. I wasn't sure if I should have called, but I was starting to lose it." She mumbled.

Tightening his grip on her, Lance pulled back to tear a deeper hole into her face with the beam in his eyes. "To say that I would have been pissed that something had happened to him and not have been informed, is an understatement."

Myah could only smirk at his comment because it didn't need a rebuttal. Everyone knew that Lance had a terrible temper when provoked. Since she was eight years younger than him, Myah had tested it her whole life. She'd made it her business to test the bond that Micah and Lance shared with the notions of a nagging little sister. But, it all changed when she wanted to be recognized as more than a little sister by Lance. All attempts had failed, until one particular night.

Myah watched Lance interact with the mute and unresponsive Micah whose features mirrored hers. The tenderness in Lance's touch towards Micah made Myah all the more content with the decision to disrupt Lance's life and have him fly home after so many years. Per the instructions of Lance's grandmother, Myah had to contact the Red Cross, who communicated with his commanding officer to notify him of the family emergency.

From a far, Myah admired Lance's chocolate skin, clean shaven appearance and built physique. He was a chocolate god to all who dared to feast. Within an hour, the immediate family began to file into the spacious private hospital room. There were tons of hugs and kisses exchanged with the inquiries of Lance's whereabouts within the Army for the last six years. Myah's parents, Lena and Michael Johnson seemed the most interested in where their son from a different mother had gone off too.

They were the perfect couple. Lena was of Korean and African decent and Michael was seventy percent Cherokee and thirty percent African American. They were some of the prettiest, most kind hearted people that one could set eyes on. Myah took after her mother's height and Micah and Michael stood firmly at the six foot mark.

As the conversation progressed, Myah's mind drifted back to the events that occurred seven years ago; ten months before Lance ran out of her life.

Seven Years Ago—
February 14, 2007

Myah got dressed as she waited for the clock to chime 6pm. Her brother Micah was scheduled to arrive at her dorm room within an hour. Even though, he normally gave her a few extra minutes because he knew that she was a woman in her own right and time was never on her side.

Prancing between the bathroom and the bedroom of her freshmen dorm at Oakland University, Myah noticed that she missed a call. Checking her voicemail, she listened to Micah cancel their ritual Valentine's Day plans. Myah felt a wave of disappointment sweep over her. Since the age of thirteen, as long as Micah wasn't in a serious relationship, he would allow Myah to be his Valentine's date. Per her father's rules, she wasn't allowed to officially date until the age of eighteen. Their father Michael wasn't entirely a sexist, but he was stricter on Myah than Micah when it came to the dating scene, so Micah improvised.

In the midst of listening to the ending details of the voicemail, there was a knock at the door. Cradling the phone in between her shoulder and left ear, Myah opened the door without inquiring who it was. But, when Lance stood in her doorway, she hung up the phone immediately.

"What are you doing here?" She asked breathlessly, as if she had just ran a marathon.

Lance walked passed her and into the dorm room suite. "Did you get your brother's voicemail?"

Myah couldn't help but to stammer, Lance made her nervous on so many levels, but not in the way that most people would think. "Umm, Umm I didn't finish listening to it. I just heard the part that he was calling to cancel."

"Yeah, but he sent me as his back up!" Lance confirmed.

"Whhhhatttt? You don't have any hoes this year?" Myah couldn't stop herself from joking. She didn't know why, but Lance chose some of the sluttiest females to entertain.

"I don't have hoes and watch your mouth!" Lance lifted one of Myah's pillows and tossed it in her direction.

"Ah, no! I'm not a kid anymore Lance, I can cuss just like you and Micah. And to be clear, those rats you entertain are hoes, with a capital H."

Not knowing what to say, Lance shook his head as his only reply. He knew that Myah was partially right. He dealt with women that were below his standards and pay grade, but he couldn't deny that he enjoyed their company, for multiple reasons.

"How much longer are you going to be? Micah said that you two usually do dinner and a movie." Lance absently stated.

Peeking her head out of the bathroom, Myah answered. "Yes, normally we do! Do you want to change it up a bit?"

"Like what M&M?" Lance had teased her for years with the nickname because her full name was Myah Michelle Johnson. He figured it was better than calling her M.J, which is what he often called Micah.

Myah's mind was whirling, she wanted to do something different because Lance wasn't her brother. And although she had known him all of her life, he was the furthest thing from a sibling in her eyes. The way that she dreamed and lusted for him was much too inappropriate to consider Lance a relative. "I'm thinking dinner for sure, but what if we do this Jazz spot in the city? I think they have a live band tonight."

"Since when do you like or listen to Jazz?" Lance asked.

"I don't, but I know that you do! I'm willing to compromise since you gave up your intriguing night to spend it with me!" Myah taunted.

Before Lance could respond, Myah emerged out of the bathroom. She assaulted Lance's senses, dressed in a black fitted dress that stopped mid-thigh with fish- nets stockings and suede wedge heel boots that accessorized her outfit.

At a loss for words for the second time since Lance had crossed her threshold. He felt something stir that he hadn't noticed before. After 180 seconds of silence, he pinpointed it as LUST. Maybe filling in for his friend was a bad idea, because he loved him more like a brother.

Hell, he looked at Myah like a sister. A nagging ass, spoiled, bratty, sarcastic and annoying little sister. He had watched her grow up from a baby into a woman. *Damn when did she grow into a woman?* Lance was stomped. Myah had breasts, thighs, curves and an ass that didn't make you double–over, but big enough to make Lance do a double take.

Knowing that she had shocked him, Myah smiled privately. *That's what he gets for sleeping on me all these years, she giggled inwardly.* "Lance did you hear me?" Myah had to try and play it off the best way possible. Innocence was her only cover-up, so she would utilize it to her full advantage!

"Are you ready to go?" Lance questioned.

"Are you up for the Jazz spot in Greektown or no?" Myah counter asked.

"Sure." Lance had to be careful that his posture and change in breathing hadn't alarmed Myah. "Wait, how are you going to get into Greektown, you're only eighteen?"

Myah smiled a mischievous smirk that made the Grinch look like a saint while pulling the card out of her wallet. "My I.D. says that I was born December 22, 1985 instead of December 22, 1989."

Shaking his head, he propped open the door to exit her bedroom. "Your ass is something else, let's go Myah!"

Walking into the Jazz Loft in Greektown forty-five minutes later, Lance felt right at home. Myah relished in the smile that spread across his handsome mouth, reflecting the prettiest teeth Myah had ever seen on a man.

They secured a table near the window in the dimly lit establishment and relaxed into the arms of the live band that had just graced the stage. Lance pulled the chair out for Myah with his eyes glued to the musicians and his fingers drumming the back of her chair.

As soon as their waitress approached, Myah went to order a martini. Lance cut in and ordered her a large cranberry juice instead. "Not on my watch M& M, you need to be lucky that I let you out of the door with that *'sex me'* dress on."

Laughing at his uncomfortable and smug grin, Myah watched him in silence. Refocusing their attention back to the stage, the time began to speed pass as they laughed at the individuals that decorated the scenery. The sense of fashion was scarce and the clothing left little to the imagination. Uprooting from her chair, Myah extended her hand towards Lance in a gesture to dance.

Accepting her offer, Lance led Myah to the dance floor and pulled her close in his embrace. Laying her head against his chest, she could feel the hardened muscles that were hid underneath his silk shirt. Myah wasn't surprised at the condition of his body because Lance had played multiple sports in high school, including football. She understood why women constantly fell at his feet; she was just baffled because Lance didn't refute any of their advances.

By the time the band began the instrumental chorus of song two, Lance's hands slipped further down her back. Myah's nose was plastered to his chest, savoring the texture of his brown, warm skin enveloping her body. Every breath that Myah took was soft enough to distract him as her breast swayed against him, but not enough to heighten the arousal of his male anatomy.

Resting in his masculine presence, Myah made a silent truce with herself. She didn't want to fight against what she felt for Lance because she had always loved him. But, what if she made a move and he rejected her? Where would that leave them? There were times when she would purposely get dressed and comb her hair just because she knew that Lance was coming over. Of course, it was to see Micah, but Myah always found a way to make herself seen. Unfortunately, it seemed that the only way Myah ever got a response out of Lance was when she was pestering him. At eighteen years old, Myah had outgrown that phase and she didn't want Lance to tolerate her, she wanted him to love her back.

Myah crept back into her dorm room a little after midnight with Lance close on her heels. He was always a gentleman first and making sure she made it in safely was a part of that job. Before he could turn and walk back down the hallway, Myah grabbed his tie, rose on her tippy toes and pressed her breast to his.

"Whoa, M&M, chill!" Lance sputtered.

"And what if I don't want to?" She challenged.

"Then I can't help you, you're on some other shit! What is this?" Lance asked confused.

"Tell me that you don't feel it?" Myah urged.

"Feel what? All I feel is you holding my $100 shirt in a death grip!"

Myah bent her head down and when she lifted it again, that's when Lance saw that she was serious.

"Myah?" When she didn't answer him, Lance lifted her chin further up towards him with the tip of his index finger. "Baby girl, you're like a sister to me! I wouldn't dare ruin that!"

Feeling that his explanation was a load of horse shit, Myah let go of the grip that she had on him. "Maybe. But, I think it's so backwards for you to want those tramps that you have paraded around with for years and not me."

"Myah, I've known your spoiled ass your whole life. I have never thought of you in that aspect and even if I did, I wouldn't taint the relationship with your brother for a piece of pussy!"

Stepping back from the force of the verbal blow. "A piece of pussy, huh?" Myah reiterated.

"You know what I meant, Myah! Don't ruin a perfect night by picking a fight with me!" Lance exhaled.

Holding onto the back of the door handle, Myah tightened her grip. "No problem, good night!" Slamming the door in his face, Myah turned and slid down the back of the door as if she were as spineless as a ball of putty and silently cried. She made a fool out of herself and there was nothing that she could do about it.

Chapter 2

"Myah?" Lena called her daughter's name when she realized that she hadn't said a word in over thirty minutes.

"Yes Mom!" Myah refocused her eyes in her mother's direction, snapping out of the day-dream that she was mentally drowned in.

"Are you okay? I think you blanked out for a second. Have you eaten today?" Lena bombarded her daughter with questions.

"I'm okay. I think I just need some fresh air." Rising from her chair.

Lance watched in silence as he recognized the lust written all over her face and immediately he knew that in her mind, Myah had gone there. Standing, Lance placed his hand on Myah's back and offered some company. "I think I'll join you!"

"Wait!" Lena intercepted. "Have the detectives been back in here to discuss your brother's case Myah?"

"No Mom, no one has been here all day. But, I have the detective's number if you want to call him." She offered her mother.

"No!" Lena shook her head. "I guess I'll continue to wait." Lena responded as she walked over to stand by her first-born child's hospital bed.

Myah and Lance walked into the hallway and when they were out of sight, Lance grabbed her hand and constricted her escape as she tried to pull her arm away. "How about you tell me what that was about?" Lance bullied.

"You don't know me Lance! You have no idea who I am!" Myah half whispered, half yelled.

Lance pulled Myah into a small opening that led nowhere, but it was out of the view of those that were traveling the length of the hallway. "I know all there is to know about you." He whispered. "I know what makes you laugh and cry, smile and frown. And more importantly..." Lance backed Myah into the wall. "I know what makes you moan, I know what makes you cry-out and I know what makes you cum."

Pushing against his chest, Myah's breast rose and fell. "Fuck You!"

"Oh, I know Bae." Grabbing her wrist and pinning her back against the wall, he continued with the taunt. "I know what you can take and I know how much. I know when you're at your max and how close to climaxing you are." Lance slid his hand down the curve of her neck, while placing light kisses as he followed the trail of his hands. "I know when enough is enough and when I can push you just a little farther, before you tap out."

Feeling the desire spread all over her body and settling in the pit of her stomach, Myah bit his bottom lip. "Stop it, Asshole!" Lance's words caressed and arrested her just as his hands had.

Releasing her hands, Lance stepped back. "Okay... Okay!" He had worked up his own pressure. He knew he shouldn't have antagonized her, but he missed the hell out of her. He shouldn't have spent so much time away from her. He thought he was doing the right thing by leaving, but lately he wasn't so sure.

Adjusting his shirt as well as Myah's, he probed. "Tell me what they're saying about the case."

Walking back into the hallway to find a private area to talk, they sat and Myah ran her hand across her forehead to display her frustration. Lance watched her in silence; he knew this was rough on her. Micah and Myah had always been inseparable.

"They're saying that at this point, all they can conclude is that it's nothing more than a hit and run!"

"So that's it? Case closed?"

"Basically. Right now, we're more concerned with the damage that his body endured when he hit the tree. They're talking about paralysis, but they're not sure because he's not awake to tell them what he can and cannot feel." Myah's gaze shifted when she noticed the figure traveling in her direction, prompting Lance to ultimately turn as well.

"Hey Yah Yah!" The woman greeted. It was her special nickname that she called her friend.

"Andréa, this is Lance. Lance this Micah's girlfriend Andréa!" Myah made the introductions.

Extending her hand and smiling, Andréa joked. "It's nice to finally meet the infamous Lance Taylor. I've heard so much about you!"

Accepting her hand, Lance answered. "Likewise. You're the one that has Micah's heart."

"And you're the one that has Myah's heart!" Andréa confirmed.

Choking back a reply Myah walked off, leaving the two standing alone. She hadn't confided in a lot of people about her and Lance's past. But Andréa was definitely on her hit list. She didn't want Lance to think that she had been pining away for him to return.

Before Andréa was Micah's girlfriend, Andréa and Myah were roommates in college during her Junior and

Senior year. Myah was a magnet for good hearted people and before she knew it, her brother had also been drawn under Andréa's spell. Now Andréa wasn't the prettiest female Myah had ever encountered, but her big eyes and big heart had captivated the Johnson family from day one.

The on-campus apartment had housed four females, but Myah and Andréa bonded the quickest and before they knew it, they were inseparable. They shopped, ate and walked to and from class together. It was when Andréa inquired on Myah's love-life or the lack thereof, Myah exposed some of the relationship that she had with Lance. Never in a million years, did she expect Andréa to end up in the middle of the chaos by falling in love with her brother.

Myah entered into the hospital room where her parents and brother remained with Lance and Andréa following closely behind her.

"Lance how long will you be staying?" Lena inquired. "How much time did the Army give you?"

"As long as it takes!" Lance replied to Lena, but his eyes were glued to the bed. "I took some personal time off." Lance hadn't taken leave or been home in years, he had plenty of time reserved and he was readily willing to use it.

Silently, Myah took another assessment of Lance. His posture had changed, it was straight and erect and his motions and movements seemed to be calculated. He looked like the same Lance Taylor, but his eyes confirmed that he wasn't and something had changed him. Myah recognized the power and resilience behind his eyelids; they had called and demanded respect.

"Well we're definitely going to enjoy you being home." Lena scrunched her nose as she smiled at Lance, snatching Myah from her thoughts.

"Definitely." Michael chimed in agreement. "You've been gone way too long!"

Looking at Myah first and then his second set of parents. "It's good to be home!"

"Where are you staying?" Michael continued.

"I made reservations at the Marriott that's in between your house and the hospital!"

"If that becomes too costly, there is always a room for you at our home!" Michael offered.

"Thank you, I appreciate that, Pops!" Lance smiled.

The truth was that the Johnson family was all that he had besides his grandmother. She had worked long hours when he was a kid. Play dates with Micah had become more like dinner at the Johnson's table every night with sleepovers that sometimes lasted for days at a time.

Lance hadn't regretted one moment of it. It helped his widowed grandmother and he didn't have to deal with the struggles of being an only child because he had Micah and Myah. Sometimes he wished that his family situation was more along the lines of the Johnson's, but since they hadn't made a difference between the three of them, it couldn't have gotten any better than that.

"Andréa, are you staying here with Micah tonight?" Myah asked.

"Of course I am! Today's my night right or did I get the days confused again?"

"No, tonight is your night! You're right, I was just confirming because I'm headed out." Myah informed. But when she rose to her feet, her boyfriend of four years walked through the doors.

"Bryan!" Myah called out as her heart beat increased slightly. Immediately, she felt convicted. Lance had touched her more intimately within the five minutes that they spent in the hallway than the four years she had spent with Bryan.

"Hey Baby. I wanted to stop by on my way home to check on you and Micah." Bryan walked up to Myah, kissed and hugged her. He was what one would call a pretty boy. He wasn't buff, but Bryan was nicely built and it complimented his 6'4" body structure. He was brown- skinned with crisp waves that flowed gently around his head with a neatly trimmed mustache and goatee.

Bryan rendered greetings to everyone until he reached Lance. "Hey, how ya doing? I'm Bryan!" He extended his hand and stepped forward. "You look strangely familiar."

"Baby this is Lance, Micah's best-friend!" Myah tried to step in to fill the gap.

Lance extended his hand as well and stood to exit with Myah. "Yeah I was there when you took Myah to prom!"

Snapping his fingers as the comment jogged Bryan's memory. "You're absolutely correct!"

"Babe, I was just getting ready to head out. I'm exhausted and I could use some food and a shower." Myah turned her attention towards her boyfriend.

"Okay, then I'm ready when you are!" Bryan confirmed.

Avoiding eye contact with Lance, Myah gave hugs and kisses to her parents. She made her way over to the bed and kissed Micah's forehead. Whispering a joke in his ear, she swore that he smiled.

Chapter 3

Lance walked up the steps of the senior living apartment complex. He had to go and see the mother that raised him as if he were her own. After he knocked on the door that claimed her apartment number, Lance paced the hallway while he waited for the locks to turn.

"Well, if it isn't the best son in the world!" The short and fragile woman commented as she opened the door for Lance.

"And if it isn't the best mother that any son could ask for!" Lance bent down to cling to her frame, lifting her off of her feet. He always figured that he got his height and build from the father that he never had the opportunity to officially meet. Because his grandmother was awfully short.

Lance strolled through the one bedroom apartment that he made monthly payments for. The only bills his grandmother was responsible for were the utilities and groceries. He wasn't rich, but Lance earned enough wages to support himself and his grandmother Gwendolyn Taylor. He was eternally grateful for her, because if she had not stepped in at the most pivotal time in his life, he would have died.

Eventually landing on the sofa and taking off his shoes, Lance stretched out and exhaled the day's events through his wind pipes.

Glancing at his distressed appearance, Gwendolyn decided to help her grandson unwind. "Have you gone to see Micah?"

"Yes Ma'am, I just left the hospital!"

"Was Myah there as well?" Gwendolyn probed further.

"Yes Ma'am she was there as well!" Lance answered absentmindedly!

"And how did that go over? I know you haven't seen them in years!"

"Me-Ma, is there something that you're getting at?" Lance asked, feeling that his grandmothers questioning went beyond genuine concern.

"No, not exactly! I just know that they've missed you. You spent so much time with them as a child, that they were indeed an extension of your family. And when you left, I leaned on them for support."

"Support?" Lance asked confused.

"You may not have acknowledged it at the time, but you were all I had and even though you had your reasons, you left and didn't look back!" Gwen explained.

Lance bowed his head, trying to wash away the guilt that no one had let him live down! "I'm sorry Me-Ma, I'm sorry!"

"You don't have to apologize to me, I know the demons that chase you. But, maybe you should be apologizing to someone else."

"Like who?" Lance asked, trying not to become agitated at the word game that his grandmother seemed to play this afternoon.

Instead of replying Gwendolyn gave Lance the 'I'm not about to spell this shit out for you' face.

"Who?" Lance asked again.

Gwendolyn sat there silently. Sometimes she hated when Lance acted like he couldn't pick up what she was putting down.

"Me-Ma, I'm too tired to do this with you. Can you please just tell me who?" Lance begged.

"Myah!" Gwendolyn replied softly as she watched Lance's facial expressions change.

"What do you know about me and Myah?" Lance became slightly defensive.

"I know enough!"

"Me-Ma---." Lance began, but didn't know what else to say.

"She came to me after you left Lance. She was broken to say the least. Why would you cross those lines with her and then leave?" Gwen scolded.

"I left to protect her!"

"Have you told her this?"

"No and there's no reason too. She seems to be getting along just fine with Bryan!"

"Lance you've been gone six years, what did you want her to do?"

"When she came to you, what did she say?" Lance asked instead of answering the initial question presented.

"Maybe that's something you should ask her!" Gwendolyn countered.

"Ok, then what did you tell her?"

"I don't remember everything Lance that was six years ago, but I told her enough to help her heal and understand the kind of traits that you possess."

"And what kind of traits do I have Me-Ma?" Lance asked sarcastically.

"The kind that makes you run because you fear your past!" Gwen patiently explained.

Rising off of the couch, Lance walked over to his grandmother, kissed her cheek and slipped on his shoes. He announced that he was headed to his hotel room to get some sleep.

Adjusting his seat belt behind the wheel of his rental car, Lance's mind was far from tired. He knew that he had owed Myah an explanation back then, but he couldn't face her. And when he pulled himself together enough to speak to her, she wouldn't take any of his calls and at the time he wasn't willing to force her.

He wondered who else Myah had confided in during her time of need! He was going to have to deal with Myah without everyone interrupting and in the absence of her boyfriend. Once and for all, he was going to get to the bottom of the situation, no matter how painful it would be. He owed her that much!

Staring at the ceiling of his room at the Fairfield Inn Marriott in Farmington Hills, Lance couldn't get a grip on his emotions. Had he been that selfish six years ago? Did he hurt Myah more than help her or was he just trying to help himself? He couldn't help but let his mind drift!

Chapter 4
Seven Years Ago—
March 23, 2007

Lance wrestled with the events that occurred on Valentine's Day with Myah and he didn't know what to do or what to think. He had taken the last month to sort out the truth from what he perceived things to be and it was obvious that Myah cared more than he realized. All this time he thought that the teasing, fighting and arguing was apart of their relationship, but it had been more.

Lance tossed the idea of becoming intimate with Myah around in his mind week after week and it just didn't seem right. She meant more to him than sex and he admired her drive and ambition for success. Her unfiltered opinion that erupted out of her mouth and used as a weapon whenever it deemed necessary, was even admirable.

Lance had watched Myah chop down some of the most eligible bachelors from some of the wealthiest families in the Bloomfield area. He and Micah often sat and laughed, but Lance was grateful that he hadn't been on the same side as the males whom she had spiraled in her web and then devoured.

Knowing that Myah's first year as a freshmen was eagerly approaching the end, Lance needed to deal with the situation before she moved back home with her parents. It was 5:30pm when he pulled into the student parking lot at Oakland University and walked towards the freshmen dorms. If Lance remembered correctly, Myah finished with classes at 4pm on Friday's, so she should have been in her room.

He raised his trembling hand to knock on the door, but it swung open as a female who was visiting Myah tried to exit the room without paying attention. She almost stumbled into Lance's chest when he stepped aside. The student caught her balance and yelled back into the room to inform Myah that she had company.

Catching the door before it closed, Myah did everything she could to refrain from rolling her eyes at the figure that stood at her entrance. "What's up Lance? What can I do for you?" She asked dismissively.

Walking into her room, Lance whispered, "Don't be like that!" For a slight second he forgot how mean Myah could be. Some would assume it to be PMS, but Lance knew better. Myah was more than a handful, he had watched her change and develop over the last eighteen years. Micah and Lance were seven years old when Myah was born. He thought that he knew everything there was to know about her, but this new proposal had thrown him for a loop.

Myah stepped back to avoid him touching her, but it was useless because Lance backed her right into a wall. He braced both of his arms over Myah's head to block her in. "I don't think that you understand the weight of your request! How did you expect me to react, Myah?"

"I expected you to act like a twenty- six year old man!" Myah slayed. She could have been a little nicer, but she didn't want to, her feelings were still hurt.

"This has nothing to do with my age, this is bigger than that!" Lance rubbed his hands through her hair. Her hair was another thing that he loved about her; she kept herself together and when she wanted to, she conducted herself in a very sophisticated manner.

"Then tell me, what's the problem?" Myah pouted.

"The problem is that you're my best-friend's sister. I've known you your entire life and sex doesn't perfect relationships like ours, it alters it. If this goes bad Myah, I could lose you and Micah and besides Me-Ma, y'all are all I got."

Myah placed her hands on Lance's chest as she witnessed the vulnerability flash across his face. She understood where he was coming from, but she had fantasized about him for the last ten years and she couldn't see herself being with anyone else.

When Lance came to hang with Micah, Myah would make sure that her hair was impeccable and that her jeans clung tightly to the curves that had blossomed over time. "Okay, can we compromise?" Myah was caving.

"What's your version of compromising?" Lance asked suspiciously.

"I want you to kiss me!" Myah confessed, but Lance remained silent. "And if you don't feel anything, I'll discard my crush as if it never existed."

Lance was mowing it over in his mind. He didn't want to touch any of her body. His feelings were completely raw and it was still new to him that his body responded to her outfit on Valentines' Day. Yet, he was curious to see what would become of the kiss.

Lance lowered his face over Myah's to brush his lips over hers, almost teasing her before allowing his lips to settle on hers. Myah was the first one to open her mouth to advance the kiss and Lance answered the call of the pursuit. Leaning his body into Myah, he felt the desire on both ends and he was lost. Lifting her to meet his height and length, Myah wrapped her legs around his waist and he gripped her thighs to acknowledge the heat radiating off of them.

Prying his lips from hers, Lance needed a minute to think. "We can't do this! Not like this!"

"Then like what? Because you definitely just passed the test with flying colors."

"Myah the difference between your feelings and mine is that I wasn't aware of them."

"Okay, well consider yourself aware." She argued.

Lance lowered her back to the ground with his forehead pressing against hers in an attempt to gain control of the situation, but his heart was racing.

Myah placed her hand over his heart. "You won't regret it, I promise!"

"And what if I fuck this up Myah? What if we mess this up? I'm not willing to risk Micah's friendship. I'm not willing to lose either one of you!"

Pressing her lips back to his, she gave him her word. "Everything's going to be fine, I promise!"

Deepening the kiss before pulling away, Lance responded. "I made reservations at the Hyatt on Opdyke. If we get there and you change your mind then I'm okay with that!"

Walking passed Lance to pack a bag, Myah had a ton of thoughts running through her mind. Were they really going to do this? She was excited and scared, but she wouldn't trust anyone else with her gift. Even if this didn't work out, she would do all that she could to move on without making everything complicated.

When they pulled up to the Hyatt twenty minutes later, Lance looked over at Myah and asked. "You okay? You sure this is what you want to do?"

Meeting his gaze, she grinned. "I'm sure, are you sure?"

"I don't think I could ever be so certain about something that has the potential to be life altering." He confessed.

"I don't want you to think that you're doing me a favor. Do you at least desire to be with me? To be inside of me?" Myah argued softly.

"Do you think we'd be here if I didn't? Do you think I would have gone through so much trouble to make sure that this night was unlike any other?" Lance quizzed.

Before Lance could open the door to the hotel room, Myah pulled him aside and pinned him against the wall. "You promise to be gentle, right?"

Lance caressed the side of Myah's face. "I promise Baby!"

"And you promise to go slow, right?"

"If you're having second thoughts, M&M its cool Baby, we can go!"

"I'm not, I just wanted to make sure because once we get to the bed the talking would be eliminated."

"I promise that it's going to be everything that you've ever wanted and everything you've ever dreamed of! I promise to make sure that you don't regret one second while you're here with me tonight." Lance assured.

Walking into the hotel room, Myah was flabbergasted. The rose petals decorated the hotel floor and along the hot tub that was built into the middle of the room's floor as it made a path towards the entry of the doorway. Myah turned around, rose on her tippy toes and initiated a kiss that took them to the place of no return.

Chapter 5

Lance decided to head to the hospital when he woke the next morning. Today, was one of those days that he could have used his best-friend's wisdom. It was rare that he hid information from him because Micah always helped Lance think logically regarding any situation. Although, Lance and Myah were never a subject that he broached with Micah. He would give hypothetical situations without leading anyone to believe the woman that he referred to was indeed Myah.

Lance walked thru the doors that were assigned to Micah Johnson and came face to face with Andréa. "Good Morning!" Lance decided to speak first.

"Good Morning Lance. I thought Myah was coming to relieve me this morning?" Andréa asked confused.

"I'm sure she will. I just wanted to come and sit with him. Maybe chat with him for a little bit!"

Gathering her belongings, Andréa gave him a sad smile. "You know Just as well as I do that he's a fighter and I have nothing but Faith that he's going to be just fine. If anything changes, the nurses have my number."

"Okay." Lance agreed as Andréa walked out of the door. Before he could open his mouth to greet his best-friend that was more like a brother, Myah walked into the room.

"Oh no dammit, I can't deal with you this early in the morning." Myah threw her hands up in the air because he had tormented her in her sleep lastnight, resulting in a restless night.

"Well you're the person that we've been waiting on! I was just about to have a one-sided dialogue with my bro." Lance pointed towards a mummified Micah.

"You're still silly as hell, I see!"

"Bae we need to talk!" Lance went right in for the kill, taking the playfulness out of his voice.

"No we don't and stop calling me Bae. I have a man and I'm sure you found a skank in Texas whom you use the term "Bae" loosely with." Myah barked.

"So you got with Bryan, huh? I see you didn't waste any time replacing me!"

Myah walked as calmly as she could over to Lance and bent over to stare eye-level with him. "You have a lot of nerve Asshole to sit here like I left you when it was the other way around. If I were you, I'd try your best not to piss me off because you aren't the only person with a nasty attitude." Her caramel skin was beginning to turn rosy red. "You wanna talk to your bro? Good, consider yourself officially on duty."

Myah spun on her heels and left the room just as quickly as she'd come.

Racing back into the mid-March weather, the cold air stung her face. You would have thought that as the years progressed the weather would have gotten better, but 2014 had proven her wrong. Michigan was still the mitten state and spring was not around the corner.

Myah was trying her hardest not to break down; she never understood why Lance got under her skin so badly. Her emotions forced her to evaluate herself because she was still frustrated about the past, it was done with and she had to move on. Myah needed to accept that she couldn't right the wrongs and she couldn't fix, alter or reverse the past.

Sitting behind the wheel of her Dodge Charger, her heart was pounding and she felt the last bit of control seeping through her pores. She didn't have anywhere to go or anyone to talk too, except one person. The one person who had been there to console and guide her, was also the same person that would never judge her or the situation.

Myah turned the key in the ignition and pulled the car out of the West Bloomfield Henry Ford Hospital parking lot. She drove as fast as she could until she reached the entrance of the senior citizen living facility. Myah couldn't seem to get through the doors and to the elevators fast enough; she needed to get to Gwendolyn as soon as possible.

Myah knocked on the door with fast repetitive reps, bruising her knuckles. The thirty seconds that it took Gwendolyn to get to the door, seemed like twenty minutes to Myah as she started to hyperventilate. "Me-Ma, please open the door, I need you!" Myah was sobbing when the door finally opened.

"Oh Myah, what's the matter? Why didn't you use your key?" Gwen stepped into the hallway as Myah's head fell into the crook of her neck. "Please tell me it's not your brother!" She pleaded.

Myah didn't raise her head; she could only shake it NO while Gwen continued to hold her. She didn't have the strength, hell she couldn't even remember that Gwen had given her a key to come and go as she pleased.

Sweetly Gwen whispered, "Come on in the house honey, I can't hold you up too much longer in the hallway."

Myah wasn't thinking. "Me-Ma, I'm so sorry, I'm much too heavy to unload my weight on you." Myah weighed about 160lbs, but Gwen was only 120lbs and fifty years older as well. Walking in the house behind Gwen, Myah tried to get herself together. She began running her hands through her short jet black hair that was streaked with burnt orange highlights. Myah wiped the tears that stained her brown cheeks that had turned a deep red because of the frustration and crying.

As they sat in the nook of the kitchen area, Gwen waited patiently until Myah was ready. She busied herself by making tea to settle Myah's nerves and offer her some kind of peace. The look of anguish on her face confirmed that the dam had finally broken with Lance and if they weren't careful, the neatly kept secret would soon be out and aired for all to view.

Myah took a deep breath as she placed her back against the chair. She was trying to gather her thoughts, but couldn't seem to figure out where to start. She normally came to visit Gwen at least once a week and she trained herself to limit or avoid conversations about Lance during her stay. But today, all bets were off the table and if she didn't talk now, she was bound to go ape-shit crazy. "I walked into the hospital today and Lance was already there." She paused. "He said we needed to talk and I went crazy on him. I mean I don't know why, it was so dramatic of me, but I couldn't control it."

Myah took another deep breath and continued when Gwen remained silent. "Me-Ma, I thought I could handle him being here, but I think I was wrong. There is just so much that's unresolved between us."

"Maybe you should hear him out Myah. I think you two have grown and matured and now you can discuss things like adults. The way it should have been handled six years ago." Gwen offered.

"Me-Ma, you say it like it's my fault! He left, without as much as a goodbye, what was I suppose to do?"

"I'm not taking sides and I'm not pointing blame. But once he explains himself, then find it in your heart to forgive him." Gwen put her hand up to stop Myah from interrupting her. "And then tell him about the baby so that he can forgive you and then you can forgive yourself."

Myah straightened her posture. "What makes you think I haven't forgiven myself?"

"Call it intuition." Gwen smirked. "I'm not just a Mother, but I'm a Grandmother as well. I look right passed the mouth and I answer to the eyes of the soul. You have to get up before the sunlight to fool Me-Ma darling." Gwen rubbed her hand over Myah's cheeks.

Myah moved her hand to cover Gwen's as she rested her head in the palms of their hands. Before she could pretend that Gwen's words hadn't pierced her in a manner that exposed the part of her that she hid so well from everyone around her, the tears fell.

Myah couldn't remember how many nights in her dorm room she had cried. But no matter how rough the night had been, she operated on fumes to get through the class schedule of her sophomore year. During the day, she attended classes, went to tutoring, completed research in the library and at night, she locked herself in her dorm and cried. She cried because she missed and needed Lance, but he wasn't there.

Myah found herself crying when she came across couples with babies, couples displaying affection in public or just pregnant women period. So to avoid the crying spells and embarrassment, she hid in her room. She often found herself avoiding food and every pound that she gained during her freshmen year, quickly disappeared.

When she composed herself to speak, Myah whispered, "I wanted that baby Me-Ma. I loved Lance and I wanted our baby!"

Gwen took a deep breath, "I assured you that you could have kept it and everything would have been alright. But I couldn't make that decision for you!"

"Me-Ma, how was I supposed to keep a baby without shaming my parents and dropping out of school to raise it?"

"People do it all the time. They have babies and they continue school. It just makes you grow up faster than your peers, that is all." Gwen reassured.

"And what about Lance and I? Everyone would have known, it would have ruined his relationship with my family and I didn't want to risk that." She sighed. "I promised him that I wouldn't let that happen!"

"Well here you two are six years later. He's thirty two and you're twenty five. Whatever you decide to do from this point on, will only matter to you two."

Myah rose to her feet, she couldn't take anymore today. "Me-Ma I'm tired, I just want to go lay down." Leaning over to hug and kiss Gwen, Myah turned out of the kitchen and stumbled into Lance.

Lance walked so quietly into the house that they hadn't noticed his presence. From the expression on his face, Myah knew that he heard most, if not all of the conversation.

Myah spoke first. "Who's sitting with Micah?"

Lance paused before responding, "Your parents!"

When Lance didn't further his explanation Myah let it go. "Ok!" She moved to walk around him when he grabbed her arm.

The energy that he transferred in his grip, forced Myah to look at him and without warning the tears flooded her eyes, blinding her from seeing. "Please, don't!" She begged.

Lance pulled her into his arms, forcing her to let him hold her. "Baby, I'm sorry!" He whispered.

The three words broke the last strand that had been holding her together and Myah collapsed in his arms. She cried for what seemed like hours. She wept for all the years that she spent without him and she cried as she released the weight of aborting their baby. Myah continued to cry because she loved him and wasn't sure that she could leave Bryan to finish what she and Lance started so long ago.

The ugly truth was that so many years had passed. Lance didn't know the woman she had grown to become and she didn't know what kind of man Lance, was now. Would they still like each other? Could they still love each other? Did they even want the same things?

Myah pulled out of Lance's embrace as he dried her face with the palm of his large hands and bent down to place his lips on top of hers. Myah didn't deepen the kiss and neither did he and through a mutual agreement, they drew a silent truce.

Myah broke the kiss first and mumbled, "When I'm ready, then I'll come to you!"

Lance let her go and Myah walked out the door.

Chapter 6

Monday morning Myah walked into her graduate class, drained. She spent the entire weekend hiding in her one bedroom apartment. This was the first time she had appreciated the fact that she didn't live with Bryan. He slept over and visited, but nothing too permanent was the route that Myah chose to take.

Myah locked herself in the house with minimal conversation with her parents or Bryan. She needed time to think and space to finish letting her dirty laundry hang before she went back to pretending that everything was normal and that her life didn't reek of wrinkles.

Lance was embodying every sense that she owned and she couldn't help but selfishly think of herself while her brother continued to lie unconscious in the hospital. The only saving-grace was that the doctors had removed the ventilator to ensure that Micah could breathe on his own and indeed, he could.

Once Myah secured her favorite seat near the window towards the back of the classroom, she allowed herself to relax. She welcomed the graduate family communications class presence and waited to absorb all of the wisdom that her professor had to offer during the session.

Basking in the ambiance, Myah put her head down on the table to soak up the last twenty minutes before class began. Within five minutes she felt a body plop down in the chair next to her. The Jimmy Choo fragrance that her friend wore regularly gave away her identity.

Dreadfully lifting her head, she noticed the same weariness that she felt reflected on Deja's face and she knew that "men trouble" was lingering in the air. Deja and Myah had grown close through the Counseling Masters Program. Master's programs were slightly different than Bachelor's, but the same logic remained. Whoever you entered a program with, you remained in the same classes with them leading to graduation as long as they didn't quit or flunk out.

If Myah hadn't been secure in her own skin, she would have been insanely jealous of Deja and a friendship would have been impossible. Deja was a 5'7" thin frame, mixed brown skinned girl with curly, long, flawless hair that reached the center of her back when it was untamed. She reminded Myah of Zoe Saldana from the movie *Columbiana*.

"Hey Deja, Honey! What's going on?" Maya inquired.

"Nothing, I don't want to dump my problems on you, you've got your plate full already." Deja confessed. She and Myah had spoken outside of class and Deja was more than aware of the critical condition that Micah was in.

"Oh no, please I insist, I could use the distraction." Myah persuaded.

Deja lowered her head and when she lifted it again, tears stained her face.

"Oh no, Deja, don't cry." Myah comforted. "What's the matter?"

"He's getting married!" Deja blurted, "I don't know what to do, how to feel or what to say!"

"Who's getting married?" Myah asked confused.

"David!!!" She sniffled.

"Who the hell is David, Deja?"

"Well, technically he's my brother-in-law!"

"Brother in law?" Myah asked, more baffled now than ever. "Is he related to your husband?"

"No not my husband, are you crazy? That would be estúpida." Deja yelled, "He's my sister's husband's, brother."

"I don't understand why you would care that your brother-in-law is getting married. You should be nice and buy him a gift." Myah encouraged.

"Are you loca, Chica? He's my first love. I've known him for the last seventeen years, since I was ten years old." Deja confessed.

"But you're already married, Deja. I don't know if you get to be mad or upset because you've already made your choice." Myah reasoned.

"When I got married, we weren't even on speaking terms, but David showed up at my house three days before my wedding trying to reason with me not to marry Jason."

"So why did you, if David is who you really love?" Maya asked.

"Its not that I don't love Jason, it's not even that I'm not happy with Jason. It's just different with David." Deja sighed. "We've never had sex or even seen each other naked, but I love him. There's no real sexual chemistry between us, but there's a pull that I feel when I'm away from him."

"Maybe you should have a conversation with David." Myah suggested.

"I can't."

"Why not?" She questioned.

"For one, I talk in my sleep." Deja whined.

"What do you mean you talk in your sleep?"

"I have full blown conversations in my sleep, where I repeat anything that weighs too heavily on my conscious."

Myah burst out laughing, "What the fuuucccckkkk!"

"It's honestly not funny, Punta!" Deja cursed.

Holding her hands up in defense."Lo Siento!" Myah apologized jokingly. "And what's for two?"

"For two," Deja paused. "I don't know how to express my feelings to him in person!"

"Why not?"

"Because he turns me into that ten year old girl again." Deja sighed. "I become this shy, insecure adolescent who knows what she wants, but too terrified to go after it."

"Well you need to figure this out. The last thing you need to do is start living and sleeping with one man, while dreaming and lusting after another." Myah warned.

"It's crazy because I don't know if I could be with him because he's such a womanizer. But, then I always reason that he would never be that way with me. I think it's the fear of the unknown that holds me back." Deja sighed again. "The matters of the heart are so tricky."

"It's more like they're deceitfully wicked." Myah knew the game all too well.

"Si, Muy Mal, Chica!"

Myah agreed, she knew it was all bad. Deja was a certified bi-lingual major in undergrad, but she was considerate enough to only use words that she was certain that Myah understood.

The remainder of the class period, Myah and Deja were submersed into their own private thoughts. Myah needed to have a conversation with Lance and Deja needed to make peace with David before Jason found out.

Chapter 7

It had been several days before Lance decided to go looking for Myah. He had tried giving her some space, but there were some imperative things that they needed to discuss. The word "Baby" had continuously rang in his ears for days, leaving him unable to eat or sleep as the guilt swallowed him up, day in and day out.

Gwen had previously told him during their monthly conversations about the Johnson's family restaurant that had opened several years prior. Michael Johnson had been a plant supervisor for Ford when Micah and Myah were growing up. He retired, using his stocks and bonds to create a franchise.

Lance pulled his car into the soul food parking lot off of Northwestern Hwy and 12 mile. He knew that this was one place that Myah was sure to be. Since Myah was a family person, Lance figured that she didn't have a regular job because she invested most of her time here. It went without saying that the restaurant was successful, so Myah didn't need to seek additional employment.

When he walked into the establishment, the hostess greeted him. "Welcome to Micah's Soul Food!"

"Thank you!" Lance smiled as he leaned towards the podium. "I'm looking for Myah Johnson, is she here?"

"Sure, wait one second while I get her." The hostess disappeared into the kitchen and within a matter of seconds she returned with Myah in tow.

Lance couldn't help notice that Myah's smile diminished when she confirmed the identity of her guest. Without a word, Myah grabbed his hand and led him towards the office. She wasn't surprised that he had searched her out. She knew him well enough to know that he had given her a deadline and by his abrupt appearance, she had obviously exceeded it.

Pulling him into the office, Myah let go of Lance's hand. When she turned to face him, her only reply was, "Hey!"

Lance was silent as he used his right thumb to brush over the bags that had formed under her eyes. To a normal individual they would have missed it, but he knew her. He had memorized every facial expression down to the hairs on her head. From their first encounter at the hospital the week before, up until moments ago, he knew that she hadn't been sleeping.

Myah relaxed in the feel of his hands. "It doesn't look like you've had much sleep either." She mocked the same movements of her thumb under his eyes just as Lance had done to her.

Lance bent down and replaced his thumb with his lips; he kissed her right eye and then her left. He moved to her nose and then proceeded towards her right cheek and then her left. But when he tried to kiss her lips, Myah moved so that he caught her chin.

"I can't think when you're touching and kissing on me, it's quite distracting." Myah admitted.

"I can respect that!" He paused briefly, before proceeding. "Can you tell me about our baby?"

Myah recoiled as if he had slapped her; she shook her head before actually blurting out the word, "NO!" For additional emphasis, she repeated it. "Hell No!"

And that's when she saw it! Lance straightened his posture and shielded his emotions when he dimmed the glow in his eyes. Myah recognized it as a self preservation mechanism. She hadn't given him what he wanted and in all actuality there was nothing that he could do about it.

"No?" He questioned. "Is this a game to you?" He stared at her stunned expression. "Do you get some kind of pleasure out of torturing me?"

If Lance hadn't been blinded by his own frustration, he would have noticed the change in Myah's complexion from the soft brown to the rosy red.

"Games?" She snarled. "Torture?" Myah had started looking around the room for her knife, she had enough of the bullshit and her only resolution was to just cut his ass. "Do you know how cold an abortion table is?" She balled up her fist. "Do you have any idea, how lonely the emotional healing process of that is? Can you imagine the bleeding and cramping associated with aborting an eleven week old baby?"

By now, Myah was hysterical. Lance went to cover her mouth to calm her, when Myah slapped him. "Don't touch me!" She growled. "Don't you dare touch me!" Myah walked passed him and out the door, leaving Lance staring at her back.

Her words had hurt him more than the stinging in his jaw. An eleven week old fetus was a baby. Lance hadn't realized the weight of his decisions until that moment. Myah was still hurting and he couldn't substitute or eliminate her pain.

That night, Lance sat alone in his hotel suite and just as he started to pace the floor, there was a knock at the door.

Peeping through the keyhole, he hesitated. "Did you come for a rematch?" He spoke loud enough for his guest to hear through the closed door.

He watched her half smile, half frown through the hole. "No, but if you don't let me in then I'm prepared to cause a scene." She announced proudly.

Opening the door, Lance smirked at her. At twenty-five years old, Myah was still a spoiled brat that resorted to extreme measures when necessary. Myah walked in and made herself at home on the bed.

"I was thinking that maybe I owed you some kind of explanation and maybe you have a right to ask some questions." Myah acknowledged.

Lance sat down next to Myah and she saw his chest exhale. "Just start from the beginning and tell me what happened."

Myah exhaled as she recalled the events that occurred seven years prior.

December 31, 2007

T he air rained with love and excitement as the Johnson's home filled with friends and family of near and far to bring in the New Year. This was the most joyous time of the year because it brought the anticipation of one year ending and another year beginning. New Year's Resolution's were comprised because it brought hope of a brand new start.

Myah went to grab a drink and join in on the festivities when Micah took her glass and replaced it with Sparkling Cider. For the life of her, she couldn't figure out what was Lance and Micah's issue with allowing her to grow up.

The relationship between her and Lance was something new and unforeseen, but she loved every moment that she spent with him. She found that being in his arms as they slept was the safest place in the whole world. He had changed her and she had gone from a girl into a woman, but Myah had changed him as well. Lance seemed more humble as if he were walking on eggshells and as of late, Myah noticed that he had pulled back from her.

There was something bothering Lance, but she couldn't put her finger on it and he hadn't been forthcoming with the information. The time that they spent together lately had been limited and the sex sessions had dwindled in number as well.

Myah followed Lance into the den that was off to the side for a moment of privacy. It had been a week since they had seen each other and two weeks since they'd made love. Myah had a few itches that needed to be scratched and soon.

She had celebrated her nineteenth birthday on the twenty-second and it seemed that her hormones had tripled in the last few weeks. She was starting to endure what she believed to be withdrawal symptoms.

"Is everything okay Lance?" Myah asked sitting next to him on the European love seat that her mother had hand selected for the smaller living area.

"I want to be honest with you Myah and I should have told you before now, but I didn't know how."

"Well, what's the matter?"

"I'm leaving and I don't know when I'm coming back!" He admitted.

"I don't think I understand Lance."

"We made a mistake Myah, we crossed some serious lines and I don't know how much longer I can keep up the charade! I'm half sleeping, avoiding Micah and the way that I feel for you is so wrong."

"Okay, then let's deal with it, but don't leave, God, please don't leave!" Myah begged.

Lance rose from the sofa and leaned over and whispered, "Its too late Baby, its too late." He walked out of the room and joined the rest of the party in the dining room.

Myah seemed to be numb when Gwen stood in the middle of the room ten minutes before the New Year and raised her glass. "I'd like to make a toast. I'd like to wish my boy nothing but the best as he joins the United States Army."

Myah watched as everyone raised their glasses in unison and at that moment she went in search of a drink. She heard her father say, "When do you leave for camp?" Lance replied, "At the end of the week." It seemed as if Myah had been hit by an oncoming train. The kitchen started spinning as she

41

heaved to catch her breath. Before she could signal for help, the room went black.

When Myah woke up, Micah was standing over her and she was in the bedroom that she utilized while on school breaks. He found her passed out on the kitchen floor and silently carried her to the bedroom to avoid stirring a fuss.

"You alright lil sis?" Micah asked concerned.

"Yeah, what happened?" Myah was still groggy.

"That's what I wanted to ask you! You've been acting weird all night and then I found you passed out on the floor." Micah stated accusingly. "Is there something that you want to tell me?"

"Nope! Is there something that you want to know?" Myah retorted.

"Nope!" Micah headed towards the door.

"Micah, do me a favor!"

"What's that?"

"If anyone asks, just tell them I wasn't feeling well." She turned over in the bed. "I think I'm going to lay here for a while."

"Sure thing!" Micah answered and then closed the door behind him.

Every day following the New Year's party, Myah seemed to become sicker. The guilt of Lance leaving had swallowed her up. Had this been her fault? Did she pressure him into their relationship and now the only escape for him was to enlist into the Army?

The guilt that Myah felt eventually turned into anger because Lance had tip-toed around for weeks without mentioning his plans. She wasn't sure if their relationship had been one-sided and she hadn't noticed the signs because of the depth of her infatuation. The questions and doubt continued to attack her because she hadn't just given Lance her body, she had given him her heart.

Myah avoided family dinners while she prepared herself to go back to her dorm and start the second half of her sophomore year. She watched Lance get into the back-seat of a taxi- cab along with the rest of her family on Friday January 4, 2008. And as simple as that he was gone.

Myah concluded her story and placed her hands in her lap as she stared at Lance. When Lance's jaw tightened, she replied, "What? You asked me a question and I answered it!"

"Bullshit. All you did was reminisce and dance around what I asked you!" He replied rudely. "When did you find out you were pregnant?"

Myah huffed and puffed, Lance wasn't making this easy on her. "I passed out in the hallway by my dorm room door. When I woke up again the on-campus police and EMS were standing over me."

Lance remained silent, so Myah continued. "I went to the hospital and they ran a bunch of tests. The blood- work showed them that I was pregnant as well as dehydrated."

Lance's features had softened a bit. At the time, she had just entered womanhood and he left her at the most pivotal time of her life. For those reasons, he was more than apologetic because he was to blame for her decision to abort the baby. He couldn't be mad that she had moved on with her life, he hadn't been there for her.

"Why did you wait until you were so far along to have the abortion Babe?" His curiosity was eating him alive and he hated to make her relive this, but he had to know. He needed to make peace with it, but first he needed clarity on all ends.

Myah moved closer to him on the bed. "I was already eight weeks when I went to the gynecologist." Yawning in between her response, Myah elaborated. "I was six weeks pregnant when you left."

"But, you had a period the month before!" Lance reasoned.

"I know. I was there!" She mused.

Lance smirked at her smart comment. He stretched out on the bed and pulled Myah further into his embrace. Kissing the top of her head he whispered, "I'm sorry M & M, for everything!"

Myah closed her eyes and kissed his chest. "I know!"

"How did you and Me-Ma get so close?"

"I'll tell you about it later!" Myah's yawn was the last thing heard in the room.

Chapter 8

W hen Myah woke, she noticed that the spot behind her was empty. She wasn't sure when or how she had fallen asleep, but she was in search of Lance when she spotted him sitting in a chair across the room.

"Is something wrong?" She whispered with the sleep still lingering in her voice.

"Everything's fine!"

"Then why are you sitting in the chair, instead of sleeping in the bed with me?"

"I don't sleep well with other people in the bed." He admitted.

"Oh so now I'm other people?" She needed clarity.

"It's not a Myah thing, it's a personal thing!" Lance partially explained.

Myah stood at the same time as Lance and leaned into him. "I'm not afraid of you. I miss you!" She gently stroked the opening of his army fatigue pants. "I miss the both of you!"

Lance stepped back to distance himself and retain the little restraint that he had left. "Myah, don't!" Watching her sleep had brought back so many emotions that he remembered running from, yet he always found himself the safest with her.

"Don't what? Don't miss you or love you or dream of you?" Myah threw her hands in the air. "Don't regret how we ended or how you left? What am I suppose to do with all of this unresolved tension between us?" She questioned.

Lance forgot how innocent Myah looked when something bothered her and she couldn't fix it. He rubbed his hand over her cheeks and she pressed her face into his hand while gently biting into his palm. Myah walked into his shadow and placed her hands on the breast of his shirt, intentionally plastering her hips into his. Myah was excited just from knowing that his erection was waiting and nothing or no one else mattered. Before Myah could initiate the kiss, Lance's mouth landed upon hers. It was like a shock of electricity that volted through their bodies as he claimed her lips, swiftly lifting her off the ground and towards the bed.

Lance didn't know if this was a good idea, but he couldn't deny that he still craved her. The only changing variable between now and back then, was their age. Laying her in the center of the bed and spreading her legs, he didn't bother to remove her thong; he simply slid it over to the side. Slipping his tongue up and down her clitoris, he moaned. "Mmmm, she still tastes the same." Probing further to open her frontal lobes so that he could see what he had been missing, he moaned again. "And she still gets wet just like I like her!" He continued tasting the sweet moisture that clung to his tongue, long after he swallowed it.

Myah couldn't believe this was happening. She had waited so long to feel him again; touch and taste him again and now he was finally here. She wrapped her legs around his shoulders and pushed her center closer to his lips for a long, yet deserving taste. She couldn't get enough of him lathering and punishing her with his tongue. Imagining someone else sampling and feasting on what was meant and created for him, was never an option for her. To stop herself from grabbing the back of his head while concurrently arching her back, Myah grabbed the sheets. "Please!" Myah begged. "Give me you!"

Lance lifted his head at the plea. He knew what she wanted, but he hoped that he could satisfy her with just oral sex. Entering her body was another element of emotions that he didn't have the time nor capacity for.

Myah saw the indecision in his eyes and knew that she needed to make a move and fast. "Please don't back down now." She whined.

Leaning back on his heels, Lance tried to put some distance between them. "Myah, we can't do this shit. You_."

She placed her hand over his mouth and switched positions with him. With his back pressed into the mattress, Myah slowly unbuttoned and then unzipped his scrubs. Myah swallowed the large lump in her throat that magically appeared out of no where. Lance's erection was so full that it was pressing against his zipper and had practically sprung forward once freed. The masculine power that his penis possessed made her mouth water. She bent her head between his thighs, with her eyes still glaring into his, she breathlessly whispered, "We Can!"

As the head of his penis slid between her lips, her teeth grazed it. At the same time, she heard him suck in a handful of air. Inching more of him into her warm and awaiting mouth, she removed every piece of indecision that resonated. Fighting to ensure that he was completely at attention, her hand slowly moved up and down. Globs of saliva dripped from her mouth onto his shaft as she initiated the game of tug of war. Myah slowly moved over his body and crawled up his frame with her legs on each side of his waist.

Bumping her forehead against his, she permitted his erection to hang in between her legs. Myah took the head and pressed it against her folds as she began to open for him, as she always had. She didn't know what made her believe that she could ride him after so much time, but she wanted this, she needed him.

When she slid down onto his dick, she paused to make sure that he understood that she remained tight just for him. Opening her eyes to find him staring into hers, Myah knew that Lance understood. She raised her hips and dropped them again with a little more force as her body fought to accept him. He was pressing against her g-spot with only two strokes and Myah was going to try for a third time, when she felt him reach up and grab the back of her neck. Forcing his lips against hers, he pumped his penis into her opening, causing her insides to quiver. With a second thrust, he whispered, "Try and move with me Baby! You feel that? Move with it Baby, move with me!"

Myah tried her hardest to keep up when the tingling feeling returned. But, instead of it starting at her feet, it was positioned in her center. "Baby!" She tightened her hold on his shoulders and moaned. "Oh God, Baby!"

"That's it. That's it. Take it Baby."

"I---- I Cant. I can't take no more!" Out of breath and slightly dizzy, Myah couldn't help but to move her hips faster as she fell onto his penis harder. It felt like she was drowning, but the closer she came to the surface, the more the pleasure began to spread.

Lance felt her body tightening around him and before she could complete the phasing that the orgasm had caused, he switched positions with her. Gripping her hips and diving deeper into her walls, he made her body accept everything that he had to offer.

Myah knew that he was repeating the act to ensure his own release, but her body couldn't help but to respond to the passion. She was gearing towards a second orgasm when her hips matched his rhythm. Interlocking her legs around his back, she caused Lance's balance and composure to slip.

Before Myah could completely arch her back, Lance lifted her from the bed with her legs still intertwined. He held the back of her neck and stroked while the desire and passion brewed. Their need bonded them together as they simultaneously came, surrendering to the energy that they created. Lance collapsed on top of Myah with both of them making a thud against the mattress.

Sprawled in between the sheets, Lance wrapped his arms around Myah with his lips caressing the structure of her ears. "Tell me why you aren't sleeping with your boyfriend?"

Being in his arms unlocked so many emotions for Myah. She knew that as soon as he entered her, he would realize that she hadn't been with anybody else. "Because I was waiting for you!"

"Myah that kind of stuff doesn't fly in normal relationships. You've been together for four years, yet you've never slept with him?"

"I mean he's not suffering." Myah rolled her eyes. "I mean we do everything except 'it.'"

"And he's satisfied with that?"

"Why does it matter Lance? I'm laying here with you!"

"I guess it doesn't. I've never found much logic in your way of thinking, but if he's not complaining then who am I to stand in the way of his happiness." Lance chuckled.

After a full sixty seconds of silence, Lance whispered, "I missed you too Bae, more than you will ever know or understand." He pulled her closer and kissed her. "And I love you, through everything, I never stopped loving you."

"I love you Mr. Taylor, I always have and I always will." Myah locked her fingers through his and drifted off to sleep.

Chapter 9

The vibrating on the dresser woke Myah from her very much needed and peaceful sleep. When she turned around, she noticed that Lance had retreated back to the chair across the room. She wasn't sure what his deal was, but she promised herself that she would get to the bottom of it.

Myah answered the phone as Andréa persisted to call. "Hey Drea, what's going on?"

"Hey Yah Yah, I need to tell you two things, okay?" Andréa informed.

"Ok, what is it?" Myah asked wearily as she silently prayed that it wasn't her brother.

"The first thing is..." Andréa faded into the background, she wasn't quite sure how to execute the instructions that were given to her.

"Is what dammit? You're worrying me!" Myah yelled into the phone.

"Your brother's awake, BUT, he doesn't want you to tell anyone!"

"Huh? This isn't making sense Andréa." Myah barked. "I'm getting dressed and I'm on my way!" She had already slid off the bed in an attempt to look for her bra and panties.

"He only wants you and Lance to come. He said he needs to talk to you both, privately!" Andréa finally explained.

"Well, why didn't you just say that then instead of the theatrics?"

Slightly offended by Myah's comments, Andréa uttered, "We'll see how much of a production with theatrics this shit will be once y'all get here!" Andréa threatened as she hung up the phone in Myah's ear.

"What's going on Myah?" Lance sat up, trying to shake off the sleepiness.

"He's awake!"

"Whose awake?" Lance asked.

"Micah, Micah's awake!" Myah slipped on her pants. "He only wants to see you and me at the hospital so hurry and get dressed, please!"

Myah and Lance walked into the Bloomfield Hospital, approximately twenty minutes later. They decided that it would be more explainable, if they showed up in separate cars.

Myah was the first one to run and hug Micah. "It's so good to have you back Big Brother!"

Micah returned her hug and shook palms with Lance. He studied the two before making the announcement. "Do you know what's funny about people who are unconscious?" Micah asked.

"No! What?" The two under surveillance answered in unison.

"The funny thing is that other people in the room never know how much or how often the patient is actually unconscious."

"What the hell are you talking about Micah?" Myah turned towards Andréa and asked, "Has the nurse been in here since he's been awake?"

Lance remained quiet because he understood Micah's point. Not because it was a man thing, but because it was a brother thing. If no one understood them, they understood each other.

"I'm talking about you and Lance!" And for emphasis he added, "Bae!"

When the room rendered silent, Micah went on. "Would either one of you care to explain the argument that you had the other day while I was trying to sleep peacefully?"

Myah's mind was whirling with all kinds of explanations for the brief spat that she and Lance had while lingering over Micah's body last week. She couldn't even laugh at his coma humor. "No, there's nothing to discuss, it's a dead issue." Out of the side of her eye, Myah noticed that Lance flinched at the mention of the word, *dead*.

"Well here's my suggestion!" Micah adjusted his body in the hospital bed, using the remote to make him more comfortable. "Get that shit together and quickly. Oh and Lance, don't start nothing else with Myah that you aren't willing to finish."

Micah had known that something was up with Myah after Lance left six years ago. The pieces of conversation that he caught during the last week, had confirmed his suspicions.

"I also suggest that you go home and bathe because you smell like sex, especially you Myah! Was it that good?" Micah harassed.

Myah looked at Andréa and then at Lance. "We are so not about to have this conversation. The next time you wake your humorous ass up from a coma, I'll be sure to wash my ass before coming." Myah got up and walked out the hospital room, leaving the other three laughing at her back.

As she disappeared down the long corridor she heard Micah's faint voice say, "Aww come here, don't leave, I was only joking M&M!"

Another week had passed and Myah was exhausted from taking turns to make sure that Micah had completed his routine therapy sessions. The doctors weren't confident enough in his condition to release him, but they were certain that Micah would make a full recovery. The ligaments in his knee were damaged and he also had fractured ribs and a shattered elbow. But he was going to live and that's all that mattered.

The paralysis testing came back negative, lifting everyone's spirits considerably. Lance and Myah had kept their distance, but Micah continued to make snide remarks that pierced like daggers. To Lance and Myah, it was a torture tactic because they weren't sure if Micah was going to 'out them' or not.

As Myah pulled into her school parking lot the following Monday, her phone chimed with Deja's picture flashing on the screen.

"Mamacita, talk to me!" Myah answered.

"Meet me at the Friday's across the street from the school, I need a drink!" Deja voiced her request and then hung up the phone without so much as a goodbye.

Myah walked towards the bar area, but before she could sit down and order herself a drink she noticed that Deja was already on her third shot that accompanied her second drink.

"Hi Boo, I see you've started without me!" Myah greeted, putting her purse down on the bars tabletop.

"You wouldn't believe the conversation that I had with that bastard!"

"Who David?" Myah predicted.

"Yes, do you know that he said that his fiancé was his second skin and his sixth sense?"

Myah was speechless, the metaphor that David had used was breath-taking and she wasn't so sure that Deja could compare to such an analysis. Normally, Myah believed in the strength of a woman and the power of the coochie. Women had an untapped ability to have anything that we wanted and that included men that were already in committed relationships. But now she wasn't so sure. "That's deep!"

"Yeah, it's deep alright." Deja chuckled. "Deep enough for the sick son of a bitch to say that he wasn't married or devoted yet so there was still time for me to fuck him instead of fight with him."

Myah's mouth flew open, shattering the doubt that she had moments before. "I'm not sure how the two correlate."

"Exactly!" Deja threw her hands up in the air at the same time that the nearby patrons turned and looked in their direction.

Myah waved at the on-lookers to ensure them that everything was fine.

Deja continued her drunken rant. "Then he asked if I could possibly co-exist with his fiancé?"

Myah raised her hand for permission to speak. "What the hell does that mean?"

"He wants me to be sister-wives with the Punta. This motherfucker is simply retarded." Deja took a swig of her third drink. "I can't believe I was tripping off of him."

"He wants a threesome?" Myah asked.

"To say the least!" Deja confirmed.

Myah had babied her drink, but she gulped down an unreasonable amount before shedding some light on the situation. "Well they say that all men have flaws and sometimes we're blinded by what one man has that we cant see what they lack. We don't see that the other man has issues as well. The issues just differ."

"Que? Repite' Por Favor, Mamacita!" Deja slurred.

Myah blew out a long breath, "Long story short, you have a good man at home. Forget David because you have all the man that you'll ever need in Jason. Sometimes we think that we've made a mistake when our fate turns out differently than we planned. But, the truth is that God was guiding us all along and we're right where we're supposed to be."

Leaving the bar, Myah followed Deja to ensure that she made it home safely. It was so ironic and frustrating how Myah could have revelations on other peoples affairs, but she couldn't seem to get her own shit together to save her life.

Chapter 10

Walking into her apartment, all Myah could think about was sleeping. But, when she reached the living room, Bryan sat quietly on her sofa.

She had been so caught up in her own world that she forgot all about Bryan. Ideally, he was just there to help pass time because she didn't love him in the same manner that she loved Lance. It was much more complicated than Deja's situation with David and Jason, yet simple at the same time. She knew who held the key to her heart.

"Hey You!" Myah walked into the living room.

"Hey You!" Bryan replied. "Do you have a minute to chat?"

"Sure, anything for you!" She smirked.

"Is it premature to feel that you've been neglecting me since Lance has been in town?"

"Huh?" Myah went to protest, but Bryan lifted his hand to stop her.

"You don't have to lie to me! Our relationship has always been open, so honesty is what we'll continue to base it on." Bryan gently corrected her.

The status of Bryan and Myah's relationship was their secret. The truth was that they were more like best-friends than lovers. Bryan considered himself to be bi-sexual, but Myah considered him to be homosexual. Bryan wouldn't admit it to the general public and Myah would never confront him on it because they served a purpose for each other.

When she needed a companion or someone to hold her, Bryan was there. And when Bryan needed a date for an event or a relationship distraction for his catholic and strict parents, then Myah had been his solution. But, she often wondered how it worked when Bryan went before his Priest. Did he often confess his love and slight obsession with the same sex or did he confess everything except that?

Myah never understood how a person could go before another person and profess their sins. Regardless of the oath or covenant Priests were sworn in by, they were still human. Myah was certain that Priests judged and condemned people to hell, left and right. Deciding that she would take her chances with Jesus, Myah encouraged Bryan to continue his religion.

Speaking of confession; Myah knew that she shouldn't have lied to Lance. Claiming that she and Bryan did everything except "*it*", was the furthest thing from the truth. Bryan and Myah had never messed around and that's partially why she believed that Bryan wasn't bi-sexual. Their situation was simply comfortable for him. But, if Bryan decided to make a move on her man, then she would kick his pretty little ass. Myah recalled the glistening in Bryan's eyes when he recognized who Lance was during the introductions at the hospital. She was more than prepared to stake her claim.

"So is this the end of us?" Bryan asked.

"What? Of course not! You're my friend and I Love you. There will always be an us!" Myah reached over and hugged Bryan.

At first glance and maybe even the second glance; most people would miss the hint of sugar that Bryan hid in his tank. Bryan carried himself in such a way that Myah knew if she ever betrayed his secret, no one would believe her.

Myah woke the next morning as a new woman. It appeared that all of her ducks were now lined in a row. Her biggest fear was Micah knowing about her past relationship with Lance. But now that it was out amongst all parties, she was a little more at ease. And although he wasn't ecstatic, Micah hadn't disowned either of them.

Ultimately, she worried about juggling her relationship with Bryan while trying to get Lance back. However, after a long night of laughing and talking with Bryan, she was confident that everyone would get what they wanted.

Knocking on Lance's hotel door, Myah was nervous because she had a proposition for him and it was simply a matter of him accepting or rejecting the offer.

She knocked a second set of knocks before she heard movement from within the room. Lance opened the door and Myah went to walk in when he blocked her. "Now's not a good time, Myah!"

Myah was just about to catch a case when she noticed the beads of sweat on his forehead and the grogginess still in his voice that accompanied the stench of morning breath. Nevertheless, Myah by-passed the obvious because something was seriously off.

"Hey! Look at me!" Myah grabbed his face, but he pushed her hand away.

"Myah, please don't touch me!"

"What the hell is going on?" She could see his pulse throbbing in his neck when she soothingly whispered, "I'm just going to touch your chest, okay?"

Myah didn't know why it wasn't in her nature to leave well enough alone, but she simply couldn't. When she placed her hand over his heart, it was racing.

As gently as she could, Myah coaxed. "Babe, let me come in. I promise not to touch you or talk if you don't want me to."

Lance knew Myah was lying; she had the gift of gab. She couldn't be quiet if someone had paid her to. But, he figured that he didn't have anything to lose but his pride, so he opened the door wider for her to enter.

Trying to stay focused, Myah went to the sofa instead of the bed this time. When Lance sat on the opposite sofa she simply stared at him. She wanted him to make the first move, because she didn't mean to force herself on him, but she couldn't walk away knowing that something was wrong.

"What do you want Myah? I'm a little short on patience this morning!" Lance blurted.

"You're also a little short on toothpaste, but I didn't come at you rudely about it!" She retorted. Myah wasn't sure why he had a stick up his ass because she was simply trying to help him.

Lance chuckled and went into the bathroom to wash his face and brush his teeth. Myah was hoping that once he returned his attitude would be more pleasant.

Walking out of the bathroom, Lance stood near the sofa that Myah was seated on. "I'm assuming that you came here for a reason, what is it Myah?"

"I did, but then I was distracted by your appearance at the door. So how about you tell me about the dreams?" She confronted.

"What dreams?"

"The nightmares that you've experienced, I'm assuming that they're re-occurring?"

Myah was more of an expert on the subject than Lance was aware, but he wasn't ready to discuss it and he wasn't sure that he wanted to confide in her. They had been a lot of things to each other, but he left some areas of his life, private.

"Not today M&M!" Lance walked towards the door and opened it for her. "Maybe some other time!"

Myah remained seated. "I have never had someone kick me out of their residence so nicely."

"Well there's a first time for everything!"

"And what if I refuse to leave?" Myah challenged.

"Then I'll take the appropriate measures to help you see your way to the door."

"I dare you!"

"Myah please stop testing me, get your things and just go. You act like it's so hard for you to understand when someone doesn't want to be bothered. You can't force your way to fit in places where you don't belong." Lance had spit the words out before he could consciously censor them.

This time Myah didn't move, but it wasn't because she was challenging his authority. She didn't move because she was appalled by his lack of tact and diplomacy. But the longer she sat, the more Lance's fury spread.

He walked over to the sofa and grabbed Myah's purse, and scooped her off the couch as if she were a baby doll. He sat her down on her feet once he passed over the threshold and into the hallway. And before she could say another word, Lance shut the door in her face.

"I've been thrown out of better places than this." She shouted.

And the only response Lance gave her was the turn of the knob as the door locked.

Just as she thought things were about to get better, they had taken a turn for the worse. Who was this asshole that had just dissed and dismissed her? Myah was totally confused. All she wanted to do was be happy and the only person that she wanted to be happy with obviously didn't feel the same way.

Chapter 11

As the April showers began to pour in, Micah's health successfully progressed. This would be his last week in the hospital and then he would begin intense therapy to regain the motion in his knee.

Andréa had called Myah to invite her for some family time in the hospital room. They had purchased a DVD player for the flat screen TV that was provided as a courtesy of the hospital. A variety of foods and snacks were hand-picked and set out for the occasion as well.

Myah had arrived right after her parents, hugging and greeting her mother and then her father.

"You've been pretty quiet lately! Is everything alright Myah?" Lena asked her daughter.

Myah wasn't surprised at the concern; annoyed, but not surprised. Her mother always had an extra sense for picking up on moods swings and life altering phases and that's why Myah kept her distance when she wasn't in a good mood.

"All is well Mom, just been a bit busy!" She replied.

"I see you've been working more hours at the restaurant lately." Her father chimed in. "I really needed the help since Micah's been here!"

"Why haven't you said anything Dad?" Myah asked.

"Because I know that you have your school work and other priorities."

"This family is my priority!" Myah walked over to her father and hugged him. "Ill be able to put in more hours during the week from here on out!"

Laying in her fathers' arms had always been Myah's favorite pastime as a kid. Her emotions were all over the place and Lance was still giving her the cold shoulder, so it felt good to be held and loved.

As the conversation died down in the room, the family could hear a male and female voice approaching. Myah recognized the man's as Lance but she couldn't place the woman's.

Two seconds later, Lance strolled in with a woman whose face matched her voice. The hair on the back of Myah's neck stood straight up as her heart rate and anxiety seemed to increase. The woman looked like model material, straight off the cover of Jet's magazine with a slight tom-boy edge.

"Hey everybody, this is Jana Edwards. She is a good friend of mine from the Army! She's in town and I wanted her to meet my family." Lance announced.

A shadow of fire flickered in Myah's eyes before dissolving.

"It's lonely out there without the Sargent watching my back!" Jana explained while admirably smiling at Lance.

Jana reached out and shook everyone's hand as Lance made personal introductions. Once he got to Myah, he paused at the tension radiating off of her and the lack oxygen that seemed to be available in the room.

"Jana, this is Myah, Micah's sister." Lance completed the introduction at the same time that Jana stretched her hand out.

Myah was conflicted on how much of an asshole that she wanted to be, so she left Jana's hand suspended in the air. She heard her father whisper, "Shake her hand!" But she ignored him.

"I'm sorry Jana, I can't shake your hand because I'm a borderline Germaphobe and it's just not in my nature to shake the hands of random people." Myah lied as nicely as she could.

"Myah!" Lance had deepened his voice to grasp Myah's attention. "Be Nice!"

"Why?" She retorted. "You're not!"

Lena interrupted, "What the hell is going on here? Myah you were not raised to act like this!"

Myah turned towards her mother. "You know what? You're right Mom. I think I should leave before I cause the family any more embarrassment."

Andréa stood in Myah's path. "Before you go, we wanted everyone together when we announced that we're having a baby!"

Myah took another deep breath. "You and Micah are having a baby?" She was starting to feel more and more light-headed.

"Yes!" Andréa confirmed.

Myah did the calculations; it had been a month since Micah's accident and they were approaching the fifth week of the hospital stay. Plus, the first month when a period is missed, it automatically places a woman at four weeks, then the week it takes to confirm the suspicions with a positive pregnancy test. So that would put her at about ten to eleven weeks. "Then you're almost eleven weeks along, right?" Myah accused rather than asked.

Andréa's mouth became dry. She knew where Myah was going with this. Andréa of all people knew about her extensive relationship with Lance and the end- result of that union. "Yes, I'm almost eleven weeks." She confirmed.

Myah gathered her rain coat and umbrella. "Well at least somebody around here gets to have a happily ever after." She turned towards Jana, "I'm sorry for being semi-rude to you; it's definitely not your fault!" Myah walked out of the hospital room with tears threatening to spill from her eyes, but she willed them not to fall. It was done and over with and she had to get a grip of herself.

She thought about running to Gwen's house, but she couldn't fix this! No one could! She couldn't tell her parents that she had carried their first grandchild or anyone else for that matter and it was starting to piss her off. She reflected on the lecture from her family communications class titled, *Family Secrets*. Family Secrets were pieces of information that one or more members held from the rest of the family. It could ultimately make or break those bonds within those relationships. In this case the only person who was breaking, was her.

Myah had been able to avoid pregnant people because she simply chose not to be around them! But what was she to do when the shit came knocking at her door? Micah had the restaurant named after him because he was not only the first born, but the only male who would be able to carry the family's name once her father passed away. And now he would be the first one to grace the Johnson family with a grandbaby.

Myah sat quietly on her Italian sofa with a box of Kleenex: a bottle of Mango Strawberry Moscato, a case of Jamaican Me Happy and a box of Biondes pizza that was untouched. She couldn't figure out if she was more upset about embarrassing herself with the limited amount of restraint that she displayed today. Or, for allowing everyone to see how tarnished and tainted she actually was.

Most people would kill to be in her position. She was a twenty-five year old woman who didn't have to work, but chose to. Every necessity that she could dream of, was met and catered too. A baby would interfere with that. Her frequent vacations with her friends would come to a halt and her sleep would evaporate immensely. She had done herself a favor by aborting the baby when she did because there was no telling what kind of life she would have been able to afford it.

The knock at the door pulled Myah out of her pity party and when she peeped through the hole, her buzz dimmed immediately.

She swung open the door quick enough to give the impression that she was mad, but slow enough so that she wouldn't aggravate her drunken state. "How'd you get my address?"

"Me-Ma." Lance hoped that she would let him in at the mention of his grandmother's name.

"Well, not today Lance, maybe another time." Myah slammed the door in his face.

Myah walked back towards her kitchen when she heard the door open and close with Lance's footsteps approaching the marble tile.

Myah marveled at his boldness. "Let me get this straight. First, you throw me out of your hotel room. Then, you show up at the hospital with Barbie and because I wasn't nice to her, you have the nerve to walk your bald-headed ass in my house uninvited?" Myah stood there with her hands on her hips and one eyebrow elevated slightly higher than the other.

"Myah she was a friend!" Lance exclaimed.

"And at one point I was like a sister to you!" She shot back. "Today I was nobody; I was nothing more than Micah's sister!"

"What do you want from me?" Lance asked wearily. He didn't know what would make her happy and he wasn't sure that he had the means or energy to give her what she needed.

"Initially I wanted to be your wife and I wanted to birth a bunch of black ashy ass babies that carried your last name. But today…" Myah paused. "Today, I just want you to leave!" She answered.

"And what if I refuse to do that?" This time, it was Lance's turn to challenge her.

"Then I guess you and Bryan can deal with that once he gets here!" She hissed and walked towards her bedroom.

Lance followed behind her and taunted. "I've brawled with some of the best of them sweetheart, but your man isn't one of them!"

"You've got a lot of nerve psycho-analyzing someone else's state of being, when you're suffocating in your own psychological battle that you're slowly loosing."

"Excuse you?"

"You're excused."

"You have no clue about me!" Lance argued.

"Then I guess you're not struggling with PTSD?" She affirmed.

"The only thing that's stressful and traumatic is every encounter that I seem to have with you lately." Lance insulted.

"Well, there's the door! No one is holding your black ass hostage! Adiós, Punto!" Myah's mini Spanish sessions with Deja were paying off.

"Oh so now you're name calling?" Lance interpreted her last sentence, quite amused.

"Lance please get out of my house!" Myah pleaded.

"You want me to leave?" Lance aggravated her further. Myah simply stared at him.

"That's a question, Bae. You want me to leave?"

"That's what I said, Lance!"

"Well I'll leave when I'm good and got damn ready and right now, I'm not ready!" Lance walked further into the bedroom and slammed Myah on the bed. He forced her legs open so that he could lay in between them while he pinned her hands above her head.

The act sent chills down her spin as she recalled the incident in the small hallway when Lance first touched her at the hospital. He claimed that he knew just what she liked and how much she liked it.

Myah watched Lance's eyes chill and then heat up again. She knew that Lance was going to kiss her and everything in her body wanted to turn her head, but she couldn't.

But instead of kissing her, Lance confessed, "I have the Post- Traumatic Stress Disorder and it stems from my time within the Army." He paused before continuing. "I have nightmares, small triggers and bouts of depression. I don't sleep in the bed with you because I don't know the limitations of it and I can't control my reactions in my sleep." Lance's breathing was elevated. "Is that what you want to know?"

"No!" She paused. "I want to know, will you let me help you?"

Chapter 12

Myah sat in the parking lot of the Southfield Public Library as she waited for Lance to pull up. She had convinced him to let her counsel him and effectively deal with the PTSD and she figured the perfect place was the library. This location was a safe haven for her, it was serene and low-key. They had private glass rooms that required two people to be in attendance at all times, but there wasn't a time frame for how long or short you were permitted to stay.

Lance pulled into the spot next to Myah and walked over to open the car door for her. They walked hand in hand into the large state of the art facility and up to the third floor. Once the librarian opened the room, Lance settled on one side of the table and Myah on the other.

"I just want to know, how are you going to help me? All things considered, you haven't obtained your degree in counseling yet!" Lance remarked.

"Just because a baby bird has yet to fly doesn't mean that it's not in his DNA to do so. He will soar because it's in his nature, it is what he was born to do." Myah quoted.

"Ok, go ahead then, counsel away." He surrendered.

"How about we start with a few simple questions?" Myah stared at Lance for confirmation.

Lance gestured his hands to tell her to proceed.

"Why did you choose the Army?"

Sitting back in the chair, Lance took a deep breath. "I joined the Army because I was mentally and emotionally drained and there was so much going on at the time. I figured what better opportunity to clear my head and see the world."

"Is that all?" Myah urged.

"I wanted to make a difference in another way besides the normal nine to five job that I had become complacent in." Lance explained.

"So you didn't leave because of me?" The thought had haunted Myah for years and she needed to know the answer."

"Myah!"

"Miss. Johnson!" Myah corrected. She was trying to keep this is as professional as possible.

Lance looked at her with mixed emotions. "Miss Johnson! I didn't leave because of you; I left to be better for you!"

Myah was at a loss for words, but she trying to keep up. "How so?"

"To me, I was mediocre and to be with someone of your caliber, I knew that I would have to bring more to the table. The Business degree that I had acquired was not enough. With your strong will and diverse personality, you needed a man and I wasn't secure in the fact that I was man enough for you."

And he had done it again, Myah was speechless. Lance had rendered her mute.

In the tiniest voice that Lance had ever witnessed, Myah said, "We were better than that. I only wanted you to love me!"

"I did love you. But it's a difference between what you wanted and what I was certain that you needed." He paused and then proceeded. "You gotta remember that I watched you grow up and the shoes that your father walked in, were large one's to fill."

Myah was trying to keep her composure, but with every confession, it was slipping. "Come here!"

"Huh?" Lance was confused.

"Please hug me!" Myah got up from her chair, crossed the table in large strides and stood in front of Lance.

When he looked up and saw the tears in her eyes, he realized that she had gotten emotional. "Aww Baby."

"I think we need a two-minute recess!" Myah insisted.

"Then bring it in Baby!" Lance had stood and ushered her into his arms. "I never would have left you if I had known that you were pregnant." He kissed her neck. "Never!"

Sobbing, Myah answered, "I'm sorry! Lance, I'm sorry!"

"Shhhh, don't do that! Its good Baby, it's all good!" Lance comforted. He pulled back and wiped both of her cheeks. "Are you going to help me or nah Bae?"

She giggled. "Yes, back to professionalism!" Settling back into her chair and placing the very expensive Fendi frames on her face, Myah continued. "What was the best thing about joining the Army?"

"I'd say that it's the diverse people that you encounter and the various lifestyles that you stumble upon. You realize how fortunate and blessed you are because it's a cold world out there!" He concluded.

"Ok so tell me, what's the worst thing that you've experienced in the Army?"

"There were two separate occasions that seem to stick the most, but there's only one that I keep dreaming about!"

"Then tell me about that one, Lance!"

"In Iraq, we were trying to become allies with the people in the land. They would warn us if our enemies were near and we would return the favor by building things for them and bringing fresh water." Lance stiffened at the flashback.

"One day while we were walking, a bomb suddenly went off. There were bodies and pieces of bodies flying in every direction. Those that were fortunate to survive had taken cover, but that's not what's disturbing. I can't let go of the flash from the bomb exploding!"

"When you see the flash, where does your mind drift to?" Myah sat up in her chair.

Lance was quiet while he was rubbed his palms together. Myah was patient until he was able to respond. "It reminds me of when I was a kid, right before I was sent to live with Me-Ma!"

Myah stiffened; Lance had never divulged the details of his childhood. "What happened before you were sent to live with Me-Ma?"

"I can still smell the stench of the dirty alley and I can see the fires lined along the wall as estranged families huddled together."

"Were you homeless Lance?"

"Shit I was a kid. It was my drug-addict mama, Trina who was homeless. I was nothing more than a tag-along." Lance eyes shimmered.

Myah could hear the distain and resentment in his tone, so she tried to tread lightly. She must have been quiet too long because Lance continued.

"This one night, Trina had walked off and left me standing near the burning cans. This woman walked over to me and smudged her dirty hands onto my face, rubbing my cheeks. She kept saying how handsome of a black boy I was and how she could give me a good home…" Lance stammered. "She dragged me over to the dumpster and pulled my pants down. She said that she had clean clothes for me and then she pulled my underwear down as well. But, before her sick ass could put her mouth on me, this man yelled from the other end of the alley."

71

Myah had officially stopped breathing, she wasn't sure what the hell she had signed up for, but this wasn't it.

"The closer he got…" Lance kept reminiscing. "The more I realized that he was a cop. He couldn't evict the people from the alley because it was public property, but he had authority to prevent crimes before they happened."

Lance brought his gaze face to face with Myah. "Bae, I remember the cop putting my clothes back together and lifting me in the air on top of his shoulders while yelling, "Whose kid is this?" He looked up at me and said, "Son, what's your name? What's your mother's name?""

Myah cut in, "How old were you?"

"I was five, Myah! And the scariest part was that no one ever came forward to claim me because Trina wasn't there!"

Myah nodded her head to show him that she understood. "So how did they get you to Me-Ma?"

Lance rubbed his head. "The cop took me to the hospital. I had scabs and sores from being dirty and laying with bugs that they automatically called social services. The social worker found Me-Ma! By then, Pop had already died, leaving Me-Ma as a widow, so it was just she and I."

Myah reached across the table for his hand. "Okay, let me tell you what I know! It's a proven fact that every event or traumatic experience that occurs up until the age of five, shapes a child's outlook. How you respond to certain things, is a reflection of your childhood."

"But, I didn't recall the incident until the explosion!"

"The flames triggered it. Often times, when something as traumatic and heart-breaking as that happens, its human nature to bury it far into the recesses of our brain. We begin to function as if it never happened."

Lance nodded as he processed the information. "So what do we do? How do we get rid of it?"

"Two things!" Myah began. "You took the first step by trusting me enough to tell me. That means that it doesn't hold you hostage anymore because you don't feel caged in by the weight of the secret."

"And the second thing?" Lance asked.

"I want you to let me try something."

"Okay, what?"

"I want you to let me sleep with you!"

"No!"

"Yes!"

"No, I always wake up sweating and breathing heavy and God knows what happens before I become conscious. No!" Lance protested.

"I want to watch you while you sleep and I'll stay awake the whole time. This is the only way to observe your sleeping patterns. Let me hold you while you sleep!" Myah reasoned.

Lance picked apart the details of her request. "If you fall asleep then I'm putting you out!"

"Deal! Meet me for dinner tomorrow. I have to work at the restaurant tonight!"

Chapter 13

Myah had begun putting in additional hours at the restaurant as she had promised. Despite their constant interactions, she hadn't talked with her parents about the hospital scene. Myah wasn't one to provoke her father's wrath so since he hadn't mentioned it, she figured that she wouldn't either.

Entering the large and elegant facility, Myah saw that Bryan was over in the corner waiting for her arrival. It had been a few days since she had seen or spoken to him. Bryan caught a glimpse of Myah and stood to greet her.

"Hey Myah, what's going on?" Bryan conversed.

"Hey you, how are you?" She answered.

"I'm okay, it seems like I see less and less of you lately."

"You aren't jealous, are you?" Myah asked.

"Of course I am, I went from seeing you everyday to every once in a while!"

"What are you proposing that I do?"

"Nothing, I just need you to be there when I call." Bryan pleaded.

"Ok I'm here now, what do you need?"

"I need a date tomorrow!"

"Tomorrow when?" Myah was starting to panic because she had made plans with Lance.

"Tomorrow afternoon around 4pm!"

Breathing a sigh of relief, Myah agreed. That would give her just enough time to meet Lance for dinner, no later than 7pm. "I want to be honest with you. How much longer do you think we can hold up this façade before my life begins to collide with your expectations?"

"I don't know, you tell me Myah?" Bryan was agitated, the last thing he needed was for Lance to be in the way."

"I think we can try and play this out as long as possible, but I'm going to have to tell Lance eventually and from now on I'll need more than 24 hours notice."

Nodding his head slowly in agreement, Bryan made a mental note. "I found someone, but I know that my family wont accept him, so for now, I need you!"

"And for now, I'm here!" Myah replied, hugging and kissing Bryan's cheek as they parted ways.

Entering the kitchen, Myah bumped into her father. "Hi Daddy!"

"Well if it isn't the rebel!" Michael fringed sarcasm.

"Rebel? What did I do?" Myah pleaded innocence.

"That shit ain't working today Princess, lets talk!" Michael led Myah to the private office, leaving the door open so that the staff could find them, if necessary. "Have a seat, Myah!"

"What's up Dad?"

"You tell me!" He retorted.

"Nothing, everything's okay with me!"

"Then what's going on with you and Lance?"

"Nothing, everything's okay with us too!" Myah didn't mind, she could do this dance all day with her father. She didn't have anything but time.

"Myah in about two seconds, I'm going to lose it. If you think I brought you in here because I'm old and senile, then you aren't as bright as I thought you were." Her father insulted.

Myah raised her hand for a chance to speak.

"Put your damn hand down. I tried to give you a chance to speak, but you forfeited it." Michael began to pace the floor. "Let me be more direct with you since my subtle approach isn't working!" He turned and faced Myah. "How long has this "thing" been going on between you and Lance?"

"I'm not sure what you mean?" Myah was trying to hold out as long as possible, but her father seemed to have her under a microscope.

"Are you two sleeping together?" Michael redirected his question.

Myah was as still as a statue. Her father had to be out of his mind if he thought she was going to answer his question. So she sat there mute.

"Myah I would think carefully before you respond. And let me assure you that anytime someone asks you a question, 9 times out of 10 they already know the answer."

"Well if you know the answer then there's no reason for me to respond to the question." Myah retorted. Myah had never seen her father so adamant and she was sure the rope that he had given her was wearing thin. She was debating if she should unload the weight of their secret or if she could continue to parade around living a lie.

She chose the latter. "I was grown when the relationship began and it was my idea. Lance was hesitant and cautious, while I was more of a rebel as you called me. I hope this explanation is satisfactory for you because the details of the relationship are not up for discussion."

"Thank you for the partial truth! I've watched how you've interacted with him for a long time. I've also watched how naïve he was towards your advances." Michael explained.

Myah went to interrupt him, but her father shh'ed her.

"I was a man before I was your father. I'm also wise enough to know that when a woman wants something bad enough; there's not anyone or anything that can stop her from getting it or getting even." Michael smirked. "Your mother saw this coming much sooner than I did, clearly I was in denial!"

"Mommy knows too?" Myah was embarrassed. This had been her secret for so long that she considered going to her grave with it.

"Does Mommy know!" Michael sarcastically replied. "Your mother knows everything, even the things that she deems unnecessary to share with me. I personally believe that she knows how deep your relationship with Lance goes, but I'm not interested in the details."

Myah had seen it many times in her field of expertise. Fathers that were present in the home were normally left in the dark about issues surrounding their daughters. And if fathers were informed, typically they were the last ones to find out.

Michael saw Myah's attention divert. "So do you still love him?"

Myah wasn't comfortable having this discussion with her father, but she respected that he saw her as a woman first and his daughter second. "Yes!"

Before Michael could respond, his eyes caught ahold of Lance's as he entered the room. "And I love her too!"

Myah turned around in the chair, coming face to face with Lance. She was confused on why he was there; they weren't scheduled for dinner until tomorrow.

Michael sat down on the front edge of the computer desk and folded his arms. Lance was two inches taller than him, but he was still a father figure to the young man and he still demanded a level of respect.

Lance took the initiative of dismissing Myah. "Myah could you give your father and I some privacy?"

Myah rose from the chair. Normally she would have been irritated at the men for barking commands at her and bossing her around, but today she figured that she'd harbor her protest.

"And shut the door behind you!" Her father ordered.

Chapter 14

Myah hadn't slept at all, she had called Lance once she departed the restaurant, but he hadn't returned her call. For the remainder of the night, she and her father had worked in silence and her curiosity of the conversation between the two men had peeked considerably.

She took it upon herself to stop at Lance's hotel, but when she knocked on the door, no one answered. By midnight Myah was hyperventilating, she was officially having a panic attack. The last thing she needed was for Lance to seek shelter elsewhere and have all of the progress that they'd made, vanish.

Her texts and phone calls had gone unanswered and at 12:45am, Lance responded, confirming that he would pick her up for dinner at 7:30pm. She didn't know whether to be relieved or upset because she was unsure if he had deliberately ignored her attempts to contact him or if there was another underlying issue.

The next day had gone by without a glitch; Myah had met with Bryan and his family as planned. She tried to be her polite self, but she was slightly irritated at Bryan's cowardice behavior. Myah hadn't told her parents the details of her two relationships, because it wasn't any of their business.

Unlike Bryan who hadn't told his parents because he feared that they would disapprove of his lifestyle and sexual orientation. What she needed was for Bryan to man up and soon! She didn't know how long Lance had planned to stay in town, but she promised herself that she wouldn't let him leave for another six years without taking her with him.

Bryan walked Myah to her door with a small kiss on the cheek, at the same time Lance was coming off of the elevator. The men greeted each other cordially and Lance replaced Bryan's shadow under her threshold.

"Is it safe for me to come in?" Lance whispered.

"You're early Mr. Taylor!"

"Should I go back to the car and come back in twenty minutes?" Lance smirked to compliment his sarcastic reply.

Myah grabbed Lance by his suit-tie and pulled him into her apartment and he complied by pinning Myah against the wall. "Are you going to tell me what's up with you and him or are you going to keep parading around here like you have the best relationship to ever grace the planet?"

"What exactly would you like to know?" Myah asked him.

"Are you in a relationship with him?"

"And what if I am?"

"Then it's disrespectful for me to be inside your apartment, let alone inside your body!" Lance arched his eyebrow. "Better yet, I think we should cancel the sleep study!" Lance let go of Myah's hands and walked towards the door. It wasn't until Lance had stood back at the entrance that Myah spoke up.

"You are such a bully!" She yelled.

"Then stop playing with me and answer my question Myah!" He retorted.

She huffed as she realized that she was going to have to tell Lance the contents of the relationship with Bryan much sooner than she anticipated. "No!"

"No what?" Lance contested.

"No I'm not in a relationship with him!"

"Then what is it?"

"It's an understanding. I serve a purpose in his life, just as he serves in mine!"

"And I'm assuming that the purpose is not a sexual one?"

"That's correct, that's your purpose!" She grinned as she walked near Lance. Grabbing his jacket, she guided him in the direction of her bedroom.

Lance laid his fully clothed body in between her legs as he dug circles into her exposed hips with his pelvis. He lifted the skirt and pulled down her stockings so that she could get a better feel of his covered length.

"Don't tease me, Bae. It has been weeks since you gave me some." Myah moaned.

"Well you'll have to wait a little longer Baby!"

"Why?" Myah lifted up on her elbows.

"Because you said you were going to stay awake while I slept tonight!"

"Ok..." Myah let her response fall off. "What does that have to do with sex?"

"Because Myah you're like a dude, once you get your nut, its lights out!"

Myah smacked her lips. "Well if you didn't wear me out, then sleeping would be the last thing on my mind!"

Lance was mesmerized by Myah. He inched closer to her face and kissed her mouth gently, stirring the hunger within his loins. Myah wrapped her arms around his neck and her legs around his back, deepening the kiss. If he wasn't seriously concerned for her safety while he slept then he would have made love to her. He wanted to give her everything that she wanted and more.

Breaking the kiss, Lance breathed into her mouth, "I Love You. I love the way you smile and the way you smell. I love when you're being intelligent and when you're being an asshole. I love you Myah Michelle Johnson."

Myah was speechless, she stared into his eyes and she allowed her tears to speak for her. She loved him more than he could ever realize, but she was better at show and tell. Rolling him onto his back, she slowly unbuttoned and unzipped his pants. Myah pulled her panties completely off while freeing Lance's penis. When he realized her intent, he tried to protest, but Myah slid down his shaft, snatching the words from his mouth. His only reply was a moan.

Myah slow stroked his erection, sliding him in and out of her body as she felt him tighten his hold on her waist. "Baby, you bet not!" She warned.

Lance pumped into Myah, forcing her to meet his thrust. "If you want your nut..." Lance was panting. "You better come for it, cause I'm so close Baby." He moaned as she worked her hips to tease her g-spot just enough for her body to begin to shake.

Myah threw her head back as Lance reached his hand up and clasped it around her neck. The kinky act was just enough to grant Myah the leverage she needed to send Lance into a sexual frenzy. He leaked every drop of semen that he could have offered her in a lifetime, into her body.

Jumping into the shower and moving as quickly as she could, Myah was ready to eat. Lance was right, sex not only made her sleepy, but it made her hungry too. She knew that he had said no on the sex; but how could he make a declaration of love without expecting her to appropriately respond to it?

The message that he delivered, clearly screamed, 'jump my bones'. Arriving at Micah's Soul Food, Myah requested a private booth in the low candle lit area. She could eat their food all day long; it was Lance who hadn't had the chance to sample the cooking in years. Some of the recipes came right from Lena's homemade cook book that she used as long as Myah could remember.

Sliding into the booth, Myah wanted to ask Lance about the conversation with her father, but she figured they had time to get around to that. There were some other things that she wanted to clarify before pursuing their undeclared relationship. "When are you scheduled to return to Texas?" Myah asked while looking at the menu as if she wasn't the one who had created it.

"I'm not!" Lance said loud enough for Myah to hear, but low enough for anyone to assume that he wasn't talking to anyone directly!

"What do you mean? I don't understand!" Myah scrunched her face to show her confusion. "I mean, Micah's doing better and he's back in the comfort of his home, so your mission is complete." Myah reasoned.

"It's called terminal leave!" Lance explained.

"What does that mean?"

"It means that I get to use up the rest of my reserved time and then I'm finished. I'm approaching my seventh year and that means my two terms are complete." Lance smiled at his accomplishment.

When Lance first left for the Army, he was unsure of how he was going to make it without his family. He hadn't been alone or lonely since he came to stay with Gwen at the age of five. But, Lance had grown and matured while on duty and through all the hell and high water, he had survived. Times had changed, he knew what he wanted and there was no reason to continue to run from it.

Myah was intrigued. "I thought you were going to say something like you're AWOL!"

"Hell no, people who are absent without leave bring more bad upon themselves than good. It's ultimately not worth the jail time or repercussions. Trust me, I'm on a terminal leave!"

Myah smiled. "So what are your plans now?"

"To start over here! Get me a place and some kind of civilian job and spend more time with Me-Ma and the rest of the family!" Lance rattled on.

Myah was disappointed, Lance hadn't mentioned anything about them as an exclusive couple, item or pair. When the time was right, she would address it. "Tell me about your mother!" Myah had switched back into her professional role to preserve her feelings.

Lance blew out the air that filled his jaws. "All I know about her is what I told you the other day."

"Is she still alive?" Myah questioned.

"No, Me-Ma told me that they found her body a few days after I was sent to live with her."

"How does that make you feel?"

"I'm not really affected by it because Me-Ma is all the mother that I'll ever need." Lance paused. "But, I often wonder how Trina fell so far off track because she came from such a balanced home with a mother and a father. Me-Ma and Pop weren't wealthy, but they had money. So I wonder what set of events caused her to go searching for acceptance in the streets?"

"That's a good question Lance!" Myah commented.

When the waiter brought the queso dip and tortilla chips, the conversation paused. Myah ordered turkey chops, macaroni & cheese, sweet potatoes and cornbread. Lance ordered the same, but added some greens to his diet. He knew that Myah had never been a fan of foods that were good for her, so he was going to see to it that she started eating healthier.

"So I've been thinking and making a few assessments on your behalf!" Myah admitted.

"Okay, let's hear them!"

"Your choice in women before me..." She continued, when Lance didn't interrupt her. "It's a mechanism that you used to avoid becoming seriously involved in a relationship. Consciously, you knew that those types of women would never be able to meet your expectations of a woman that was suitable for marriage."

"Okay, so…" Lance was trying not to become irritated with Myah's analysis.

"So, you left me because I affected you much more than you thought I would. You were changing and the barriers that you had in place for other women no longer applied for the kind of woman that I was."

"So what's your point, Myah?" Lance blurted.

"My point is that, I am more potent now than I was then because I am confident in who I am and what I want. So if you aren't here for the long haul then please, be so kind to tell me upfront. Because if you leave me this time, I plan to kill you and then bring your body back so that Me-Ma can bury you properly." Myah sat there with a straight face once she concluded her threat.

"Are you threatening me Miss. Johnson?" Lance was amused to say the least.

"Of course not, it's a prophesy that I pray doesn't come to pass!" Myah politely smirked.

Lance glanced at her sideways. "I got you!"

"Good!"

Chapter 15

M yah pulled the key from her apartment door as she led Lance back into the house. She felt her sleep attacking her in the worst way, but she knew that if she went to sleep now, Lance would never forgive her. So she walked into the kitchen to put on a pot of coffee.

Myah stifled a yawn as Lance followed behind her after sitting his luggage at the front door. Initially, the plan was to sleep at the hotel, but they decided that it would be better to conduct the study at her home. She went through the motions of prepping the coffee maker when Lance walked up behind her. He wrapped his hands around her waist and laid his head in the crook of her neck. "You're sleepy." He whispered.

"I'll be okay." Myah turned in his embrace.

Lance looked at her wearily.

"I promise!" She reaffirmed.

He bumped his forehead against hers and allowed it to linger there. "I don't want to wake up and you're sleep!"

"Shhh. Baby, I got you. I promise!" Myah assured him again. Carrying the coffee mug in one hand and holding Lance's hand in the other. Myah led them to the bedroom with Lance cutting off every light that decorated the walls as they walked passed. It was second nature for him to sleep in the dark.

Each had undressed quietly. Myah shuffled around before she pulled a cotton t-shirt out of her night-stand. It took Lance all of thirty seconds to realize that the t-shirt that clung to Myah's body, belonged to him. Myah caught his gaze as she smothered out the wrinkles in the shirt. Without breaking eye contact with her, Lance slid the flannel University of Michigan pajama pants on.

Myah sat on the bed, spread her thighs and patted the open space in between them.

"You want me to lay in between your thighs?" Lance questioned.

"Yes. I said I wanted to hold you while you slept. Remember?" Myah reminded him as she placed the pillow on her stomach while covering the lower half of her body.

"Myah, this doesn't look comfortable!" Lance complained.

"Oh My Sweet Baby Jesus. Lance Warren Taylor, if you don't lay your ass down then I'm going to scream!"

Lance noticed Myah's agitation and surrendered. He knew that she could get a little crazy when she was sleepy. So he climbed on the bed, pulled the pillow over her parted thighs and laid between her legs.

Myah turned on some soothing R & B and powered off the flat screen television that was mounted on her bedroom wall. Lance had favored her right leg, clasping his hands under her thigh. It was almost as if he had her leg in a loose head lock.

Myah relished in his touch as she ran her fingers through his waves. Some called them 360's because there were layers of them surrounding his whole head. She traced the crisp definition of his hair, exposing that he had just gotten a line-up.

The Army had done him some good, Myah thought to herself. It perfected his already tidy appearance and made him even more anal about his presentation to society. The reality was that Myah loved him, all of him and no amount of time had changed that. But what if she couldn't help him? What if his condition was much worse than she assumed and the lasting damage of his past was irreversible?

She continued to rub his head as her thoughts ran away with her. Throwing the comforter over his body, Myah noticed that his breathing had deepened and slowed. She placed her back against the head-board of the bed and exhaled, the hard part was over. Her initial concern was that he wouldn't feel comfortable enough to fall asleep or that he didn't trust her enough to fall asleep. Either way she was wrong and his sleep had come easily.

Myah retrieved the remote control, powered the TV back on, while activating the captions and muting the volume.

An hour had passed before Myah turned the volume on the TV up a little. The captions were beginning to make her sleepy when Lance began to fidget in his sleep. She took the movement as a sign that he was trying to get comfortable until he forcefully gripped her right thigh and held it hostage.

Myah tried to turn his body flat so that she could monitor his heart rate when his hand came up and grabbed her wrist without him ever opening his eyes. She held her breath as she recognized the gesture, he was unconscious. The manner of strength that he had while sleeping was astoundingly unbelievable. She didn't want to touch or antagonize him any further so she leaned down and whispered in his ear. "It's okay Baby, I'm here." Myah began rubbing the top of his head again. "Everything's going to be just fine."

Lance loosened his grip and Myah counted to ten. When she finished counting, his heart rate returned back to normal and he continued to sleep. She felt a small sense of accomplishment because she'd won a small battle, but she knew that there was a bigger war. Lance was going to need more help than her expertise could extend.

Pulling out her tablet, Myah began to search for treatments and solutions for patients with PTSD. When she looked up, the night sky had faded away and light peeked through the clouds. Glancing at the clock, it read 6am and her lack of sleep was starting to take its toll. It felt as if something was tugging at her and when she looked over her tablet, Lance was staring up at her.

As the familiarity and serenity lingered between the two, they smiled. Lance broke the silence, "How did I do?"

"We'll talk about it once I get some sleep!" Myah switched positions with him so that he could hold her and as soon as her head hit the pillow, she was out.

Lance had doubted a lot of things while he was away, but he was always certain that Myah was home for him. He often reasoned that it was safer to stay away from her, but she calmed his roaring sea and she lighted every dark area that tried to exist inside of him.

What kind of man would he be to let her go? He had spent six long years without her, but it was the simple fact that she wasn't unreachable that kept him alive. His time during the Army had served its purpose; he was able to put everything in perspective, gain additional experience and travel around the world. All the while fighting for his country and completely transforming from a young man into a strong minded man and if that wasn't commendable then nothing was.

When the time was right and not a moment before, he would do what he should have done years ago. He had sat down and had a conversation with Me-Ma that had cleansed some of his tarnished soul. He didn't know the man who had fathered him and he didn't remember too much about Trina, but his decision to pursue life eliminated all signs of failure. The uncertainty of where he came from tried to resonate in his DNA because of the path that his parents traveled, yet he was determined to maneuver around that.

The more time that Lance spent with Myah, he could see her healing. He had plans to make her happiness permanent, but his thoughts were suspended when his phone rang.

When Myah woke from her nap it was 1pm, the smell of coffee brewing and sausages cooking was the aroma that awakened her. Crawling out of bed, she snuck up on Lance in the kitchen. His composure was so calm that if she had scared him, she couldn't tell.

"Sit down, let me feed you!" Lance ordered calmly.

Myah sat down at the table and waited as Lance placed her plate in front of her with a cup of mouth-watering Folgers coffee.

"Last night while you were sleeping, I was doing some research and I came across these groups for soldiers to go and talk about their experiences."

"So you want me to go to group therapy?" Lance skeptically asked.

"It's called a support group and it's not just for the soldiers, but it's for their spouses as well!" Myah smiled charmingly to sell her game plan.

"I don't know Myah, its hard enough trying to tell you about it, let alone a room full of other individuals that are just as jacked up as I am!"

Myah was pouting. "Baby, I'm trying to help you, I want you to be okay!"

"Do you think there's something wrong with me because I have PTSD? I'm just as normal as you are, with your PMS having ass!" Lance insulted.

"Woah, Jackass, time out!" Myah snapped. "If I had a problem with how you were then I wouldn't be here trying to help you cope. I would have definitely stepped off already." Myah assured.

Lance was a little salty at how quickly he had gotten in his feelings; he prided himself on his restraint. "So how did I do sleeping last night?" He tried changing the subject to alter the mood.

Myah smacked her lips because he had changed the subject as if he hadn't insulted her. "Do you remember dreaming last night?"

"Briefly, but it didn't last long! In the midst of it, I heard you talking, but I couldn't make out what you were saying!" Lance admitted.

"Okay, I want us to try it a few more times. I want to see if my voice calms you every time. Then, I'd like to see how far the dream progresses if I don't say anything and continue to let you sleep." Myah needed to do more observations before giving a complete analysis. Last night seemed easy enough, but she knew that this was only the beginning. Lance needed a permanent solution, not a temporary fix.

"We'll have to do it when I come back!" He replied.

"Where are you going?"

"There are a few loose-ends that I need to tie up in Texas."

"Loose- ends?" Myah questioned.

Lance nodded.

"Does it pertain to another woman?" Myah confronted.

Lance was silent.

"Ok!" Myah sat back in her chair. "Please grab your things and leave!"

"Myah!" Lance reached his hand out to touch her, but her reflexes were faster.

Pulling back out of his grasp, Myah yelled, "Get your things and get your lying ass out of my house!"

"I haven't lied to you about anything!" Lance was somber, "I have never lied to you about anything, ever!"

"Is she pregnant?"

"No Myah!"

"Are you sure?"

"I'm positive. I have never had unprotected sex with anybody, but you!"

Turning her head at his confession, Myah was livid on the inside. She didn't know how to feel because it felt like her world was crashing down around her. Every time she thought they were making progress there was a road- block that stood in their way. "Then why are you going back?"

"Because she doesn't have anyone else and she's in the hospital. The doctor called while you were sleeping!"

"So she means that much to you that you'll go running back to her after a few months? Especially, after you left me for six years!" Myah was on the brink of tears.

"Don't do that. She's a friend Myah and I care about her. She has some health issues and the doctors believe it resulted in a stroke."

"So go. I'll help you pack." Myah got up from the table and began gathering Lance's clothes out of her bedroom and stuffing them into his bag. Without another word, she handed him the bag and before he could respond, she walked back into her bedroom and shut the door.

Lance would have tried to go after her, but once he heard the lock click, he knew that it was inevitable. So he cleaned the kitchen, left her a note and exited the apartment.

Chapter 16

The flight to Texas had been long and drawn out. Lance's mind had replayed the last few days of events as he struggled between doing the right thing and doing what would avoid a fiasco with Myah. It had been more than 24 hours and Lance hadn't heard from her, nor had she returned his call before take-off.

His heart wanted to stay with Myah, but his mind had continued to rewind the multiple times that Kenya had been there for him. He had met her at a nearby restaurant that was located near his barracks. Every night around the same time they would meet for drinks. Conversation wasn't always necessary; it was the company alone that was satisfying. After a while the relationship had turned into a mutual friendship that sometimes afforded benefits. Lance hadn't lied to Myah, he had never slept with another woman without a condom and that included Kenya.

The events of the Fort Hood killings had shaken Lance up a bit. He had never seen so many lifeless bodies that encompassed detached limbs and decapitated heads. The images alone were enough to leave him awake at night. Kenya had been generous enough to allow him to lounge on her couch with the luxury of not being alone. She didn't force him to interact with her and often she left him to his private thoughts.

Kenya had only offered her presence as a peace offering that she was available to him. If he wanted to talk, she listened and if he didn't then she never broached the subject. Unlike Myah, who never knew how to leave well-enough alone! She forced Lance to push pass his barriers and make room for her and her canning personality and he loved every piece of her.

Walking into the hospital, Lance was directed to Kenya's room by the nurse's station. Her condition was stable, but she would need supervision for the next seventy-two hours. As Lance approached the hospital bed, images of Micah laying there had surfaced and it took him a minute to adjust himself. Kenya appeared much older and the stroke had left her paralyzed on the left side of her body. The doctors weren't sure how much motion she would recover, if any.

Lance pulled a chair up next to her and held her hand. The warmth forced Kenya to slowly open her eyes and the smile that she rendered him was priceless. Her lips were a bit distorted due to the damage of the stroke, but it made his trip all the while worth it.

"I didn't think that you'd come!" Kenya whispered.

"Shhh, I'm here. You would have come for me!" Lance comforted.

"Is she mad?" Kenya asked.

"Yes, she's pretty pissed, but it will be okay!" Lance admitted. He didn't want to tell her that he couldn't stay long, so he spared her the details of his trip. During his time with Kenya, he would mention Myah and how much he had missed her. Lance never wanted to lead Kenya on, so he made it a practice to occasionally mention that his heart belonged elsewhere.

For the remainder of his stay, Lance focused on getting Kenya into a rehab facility that would be compensated by her insurance company. From day to night he spent his time contacting Kenya's employer and assisting in obtaining the medical requirements for her long-term disability claim. With each passing day, Kenya seemed to get a bit stronger. But, unfortunately the strength hadn't returned to her left side and the paralysis had caused a bit of a limp in her stride.

Lance recognized her mood changes as signs of depression as the reality of her current situation began to set in. The only person he could think to call for some advice was Myah, but when he dialed her number the phone rang and rang and rang before shifting him to the voicemail. He left her a message because he knew that she wouldn't recognize the number from the hospital phone. The signal on his Verizon phone didn't pick up well inside the hospital, so he utilized Kenya's hospital line.

Lance knew Myah well enough to comprehend that she was still pissed and even if he had called with his cell number, she still wouldn't have answered. She was one of the most stubborn people that he had ever encountered, but it made the impression that she left on people just that much more effective. Myah was one of those people that you would never forget once you interacted with her. The family joke was that she was one of a kind and not in a good way.

Kenya had started therapy in the hospital and Lance had accompanied her to every appointment as her own personal cheerleader. His goal was to have her situated in a rehabilitation facility by the end of the following week and then back on a plane by the end of that following day. As the sun had set and the night crept in, Lance's mind drifted.

He replayed the conversation that he had with Myah's father the day he intruded on them at the restaurant. Michael, who was more than a father figure had given him everything except the third degree.

Lance had watched Myah walk out of the office and shut the door behind her when he turned his attention back to Michael. "Mr. Johnson, first of all let me say that I would never disrespect you or your wife by preying on your daughter. What happened between Myah and I should have never happened, but I can't take that back."

"If you could take it back, would you?" Michael had asked.

Lance thought quietly. "I am apologetic for the way things happened, but I am not sorry that it happened. I love Myah and that is the truth, sir."

"How much do you love Myah?" Michael had challenged. This wasn't a regular girl that they were conversing about, this was his daughter.

"Enough to marry her if you were to give me your blessings!" Lance declared.

The two men sat staring at each other. Lance couldn't make out the expression that Michael had on his face, so the best thing was for him not to speak until Michael had.

Kenya's nurse walked into the hospital room and disheveled the flashback that Lance was having. It was time for the shift change among the nurses and the staff from the night before had returned. Kenya hadn't done much talking over the last few days. She admitted that it was a bit uncomfortable for her considering the circumstances and Lance understood.

Lance figured that she was a bit embarrassed because Kenya had always prided herself on her appearance and now it was out of her control. With the help of the hospital officials, Lance was able to secure Kenya a private room in the best rehab establishment within the county. They would ensure that she gained some independence during her stay so that she would be able to lead as much of a normal life as possible.

When it was time for Lance to leave he wanted to have a clear conscious. He would be content in knowing that he had done everything that was humanly possible, to ensure that Kenya would be well-cared for. Yes, he cared about her, but not with the magnitude that he cared for Myah. Soon it would be time for him to return to his life and home in Michigan and he needed everything in place.

Chapter 17

Two weeks had gone by and Myah remained secluded. She couldn't believe how gullible she had been, thinking that they could pick up where they had left off. The excitement that their happily ever after had finally manifested, was short lived.

Myah was a walking robot; she had missed a week of class because the wound was still too fresh. She didn't want to talk and she didn't want to explain anything to anyone, so she stayed home. Myah's only reason for going to class last week was to complete her final presentation on family genetics. It was the last day of class and Déjà hadn't showed up, but Myah didn't feel like calling her, so after an hour, Myah left.

Gwen had called several times, but Myah had sent her to voicemail because another Lance session was not going to help heal her this time. And if Lance knew what was good for him, he'd simply stay put in Texas because she didn't want him anymore.

Micah was up and walking and there were plenty of staff on duty to help with the restaurant, so Myah avoided her parents. She could have put on an act as if she was okay to eliminate the gossip being produced by her family, but luckily she didn't give one shit, let alone two.

She assumed that Andréa's belly was growing everyday, so she shunned her as well. It wasn't that she disliked her per se; she just didn't care for the fact that they were having a baby. Bryan had come over unannounced the night before, explaining that he finally found the courage to sit and talk with his parents and although they weren't thrilled, they still loved him.

The catholic community saw same-sex interactions as unlawful and a contamination to children who grew up under the practice. Gratefully, Bryan's parents were content with how they raised their son. At the end of the day, the decision of how he wanted to live his life was Bryan's alone. It seemed that everyone was getting everything that they wanted except for Myah and that truth alone had made her stay in hiding.

Glancing at her phone, Myah noticed that she had a missed call from Gwen, but this time she had left a message. Pressing in her code to access the voicemail box, Myah heard the message and immediately felt guilty. Gwen had called to tell her that she hadn't been feeling well and there was no food in her apartment. She had left a list of items that she needed and was pleading with Myah to bring them to her.

The message shifted Myah into gear, the last thing she needed was for Gwen to be alone in her apartment sick and hungry. Myah stopped at the Meijer's on 12mile and Lahser before heading to the senior facility where Gwen was housed.

Instead of knocking on the door, Myah used her key because of the urgency in Gwen's tone. Opening the door and crossing the threshold, Myah yelled, "Me-Ma, I'm here, its Myah!" Myah continued to walk through the apartment until she walked into the kitchen and found Gwen, Lena, Michael and Lance sitting at the table.

"Lance!" Myah whispered. "What are you doing here?" Myah turned towards Gwen before Lance could answer. "Me-Ma, I thought you told me that you were hungry and sick?"

"I called you three days ago, Myah!" Gwen explained.

Myah was immediately embarrassed. She had been so distraught by the events over the last two weeks that she hadn't paid attention to the time or date of the message. "Me-Ma, I'm so sorry! But I brought your groceries."

"Its fine, I ordered delivery those days, but you know how I dislike those fast-food restaurants. And then your mother brought me some food as well." Gwen admitted.

"Mom? Dad? Did I miss something?" Myah asked utterly confused on the family meeting that they seemed to be having.

"I think you missed your manners and your brain." Lena smirked. "This boy has got you so gone that you haven't thought about anybody or anything for two weeks. I personally feel that this relationship is unhealthy."

"Well I'm glad that it's not your relationship to personally feel any type of way about." Myah snapped.

"Myah!" Her mother and father chorused.

Myah covered her face. She needed to get a grip on her emotions because she never meant to neglect those who needed her, she just didn't want to be bothered. Myah didn't understand why everyone else couldn't understand that.

Turning her attention back to Lance and ignoring her parents, Myah spoke. "When did your disappearing ass get here?" She spat.

Lance looked around the room in an attempt to see who Myah was talking to. "Are you talking to me?" Lance questioned.

"Did I stutter?" Myah sarcastically replied.

Lance turned towards Lena, while chuckling. "Yes, I think she's definitely missing her brain!"

Myah sat the groceries down on the floor, kissed Gwen's cheek and apologized for not responding to her message sooner. Then, she turned towards Lance and gave him the middle finger as she proceeded to walk out the door.

When Myah returned home, Micah was sitting in her parking lot. She got out of her car and walked towards his vehicle.

"What's up Micah?" Myah spoke as he rolled down the window to the car. The seasons were slowly changing as the first week of May had approached. But it wasn't hot enough to wear shorts or drive around with the windows down.

"Get in the car for a second sis!" Micah requested.

Sitting in the passenger seat beside him, Myah asked. "What's up Micah? I wasn't expecting to see you today!"

"Really? Because it's been weeks since I've last seen you!" Sarcasm dripped with every word that Micah spoke.

"I've just had a lot going on." Myah responded.

"Really? Cause that sounds alot like a load of horse shit!"

"If your whole intent was to come here and insult me then please spare me, Micah!" Myah chastised.

"No, how about I be straight-forward with you, Myah!"

Myah threw her hands in the air. "Suit yourself!"

"Andréa told me about your misfortune." Micah confessed.

"My misfortune?"

"Yeah!" Micah shrugged his shoulders because the conversation made him uncomfortable.

Myah was lost and partially annoyed. "Please say what you have to say so I can retreat to my house!"

"Andréa told me about your abortion!" Micah didn't know how else to say it, tact wasn't one of his top qualities.

Myah was speechless; she thought that Andréa knew her well enough to know that information of that sort was not privy to her brother. She had seriously violated the code of friendship by pillow-talking.

Myah folded her arms across her chest. "Is that right?"

Micah continued, "I don't know the contents of what happened and I'm not going to ask you to share them, but I am going to ask you to accept my baby!"

Myah continue to stare at him. "I've been working on that Micah! I have six months to come to terms with the fact that you're going to be a father; mom and dad will be grandparents and I'll become an aunty."

"I also have another request!" Micah continued with his mental checklist.

"You sure as hell are asking for a lot these days." Myah snorted.

Micah ignored her snide remark. "I don't want you to be mad at Andréa. The only reason why she mentioned it is because she automatically became sad when you left the hospital. Instead of being excited with the news that we're expecting like she was before, she digressed."

"Well I'll be sure to let her know that all is well!" Myah kissed Micah's cheek and opened the door to exit. "I love you big bro, have a good day. I gotta go!"

Entering her front door, Myah did as she promised; she sent a text to Andréa congratulating her on the expectancy of Myah's niece or nephew.

Today was the first day that Myah had left the house in weeks; she walked into her bedroom and slid back on her pajamas because she had no intention of leaving the house again today. As far as she was concerned she could continue to sleep her life away without any interruptions.

The knock on the door caught her off guard as she drug her feet in the direction of the kitchen. She figured it was Micah coming back to list more requests of her.

As Myah swung open the door, she blurted, "Micah I already..." But to her surprise, Micah wasn't the individual standing in her doorway. "Lance what can I do for you?"

Lance bombarded his way into the house as he pushed passed Myah without saying a word and into the kitchen.

"Hello, I know you hear me talking to you!" Myah yelled at his back.

Lance turned around and asked, "Did you read the letter that I left you?"

Myah was taken back, "No, what letter?"

"And I guess you didn't see me calling you either?" Lance stared at her clueless expression.

Myah tooted her lips and shifted her eyes from side to side because she had no idea what Lance was talking about. "Lance today is the first day that I've looked at my phone in almost two weeks."

"Go and get your phone!" Lance ordered.

Myah went and grabbed the phone off the couch and handed it to Lance. When he snatched it out of her hands, she mumbled how rude he was under her breath.

Lance opened the phone and scrolled through it until he reached what he was looking for. Turning the phone around so that Myah could see, Lance yelled, "Do you see this number? Forty-eight missed calls Myah. Forty-eight Mothafu---" Lance slammed the phone on the counter and walked over to the microwave.

He grabbed the box and the paper that he left on top of the microwave and slammed it on the counter in front of Myah, whose eyes lit up.

"I left this here for you and your crazy ass left it untouched." Lance voice was shaking. He wondered why Myah hadn't called him back or even commented on the contents that he left behind. But it finally registered to him when she walked out of Me-Ma's house today with that *entitled* attitude, that she hadn't seen it.

The box made Myah's heart race, only one of two things could have been inside. A pair of earrings or an engagement ring, those were the only two options. Myah moved her hand towards the box when Lance snatched it out the way. "Read the letter first." He commanded.

"And what if I don't want to read the letter Lance? I'm sure the letter doesn't explain to me why you chose her instead of me. And why it took you two weeks to bring your narrow ass back home!"

Lance was tapping his fingers on the countertop, trying to calm his temper, but Myah was pushing it. "Would you have turned your back on Bryan?" He questioned.

"She isn't Bryan!" Myah yelled. "And I haven't fucked him, you fucked her!"

"No, she isn't Bryan, she's Kenya. And I wasn't going to turn my back on her! Yes, I slept with her, but that doesn't discard the fact that she's still a friend."

"Fuck you and your friendly ass!" Myah spat.

"All that education you got and all you're doing is cussing at me like you're ape shit crazy." Lance taunted.

"Get out!" Myah screamed. "Maybe I'll call Bryan; have him come over, sleep with him and then maybe you and I will be even."

"He's gay and you know it. He's fucking something, but it ain't no pussy!"

"Then obviously you're gay too because every time I turn around you're running from this pussy!" Myah challenged.

"Well maybe it's not us Myah, maybe it's you!" Lance cut into her.

Myah sat there with her jaws open. She had opened and closed her mouth several times in an attempt to say something, but there were no words.

Lance put the box on top of the letter and walked out of the apartment. He had said enough. Every time he argued with her, he stuck his foot in his mouth and it caused a riot. He hadn't come to fight, he was a grown ass man and he wasn't going to keep apologizing for shit that happened six years ago.

Chapter 18

Myah had slumped down to the floor. She felt like she was fighting a battle that would ultimately become the end of her. If Lance didn't want her, then she wasn't going to force herself on him. She'd simply have to move on. She had done it once and she would try to do it again. Myah had fallen asleep on the kitchen floor when she heard her front door open and close. "Lance?" She sat up and called out.

"No it's me, Myah!" Bryan walked into her view and she exhaled.

Pouting and lying back down on the floor, she whispered, "He said you don't want me because there's something wrong with me."

"Who said that? And why are you on the floor?" Bryan questioned.

"Lance said it!"

"I see you two are still at it!" Bryan said as he pulled her from her laying position on the floor and into his arms. Placing his hands under her thighs, Bryan lifted her completely off the floor and into her bedroom.

"Is it true? You'd rather be with your boyfriend because there's something wrong with me?" Myah figured that Lance knew something that she didn't because out of the last four years, Bryan had never been anything more than a gentleman with her.

Bryan sat her on the bed and looked into her eyes. "If I wanted a woman Myah, it would be you! You're an extraordinary human being with angelic characteristics. Any man would be lucky to have you in his corner."

Myah kissed his cheek as the tears flowed down her cheeks. She wasn't sure what had gotten into her, lately she cried more than a little bit. Everything Lance said got under her skin and before she knew it, her eyes were flooded with tears.

"Lay down, I'll lay here with you until you fall asleep!" Bryan offered.

Myah scrambled under the covers while Bryan turned the light off. He climbed in the bed behind her while securing his arms around her waist. At that moment, he offered Myah the peace and solace that she sought from Lance, but for now this would have to do.

When Myah woke the next morning, Bryan was still there. She moved from the bed and into the kitchen for a cup of coffee. As she passed the counter, she felt that something was off. Spinning around the kitchen, she touched the stove, cabinets and the refrigerator. When her hands finally landed on the countertops, it hit her. The box and the letter were gone.

"Bryan!" Myah yelled back into the bedroom, but it rendered silence. "Bryan!" Myah yelled again when a sleepy Bryan strolled into the kitchen.

"Yes Honey, What's the matter?"

"There was a box and a letter on the counter last night and now it's gone!" Myah was on the brink of tears. "Tell me you moved it!"

"No I didn't. He came and got it last night!"

"Who came and got it?" Myah asked with her voice elevating an octave higher.

"Lance." Bryan answered.

Myah sank down to the floor. She didn't know what to think of his actions. "Initially he left it, but I have no idea what made him come back and get it!"

"He said that you hadn't opened it, so you didn't want it!" Bryan sat down on the kitchen floor with her and Myah put her head in his lap. She felt like she was going to be sick. Leaping from the floor and turning her head towards the kitchen sink, Myah vomited. She watched as the little bit of food that she had consumed the day before, wash down the drain.

The emptiness that she felt mirrored the same loneliness that crept upon her when Lance had left six years ago. And just like then, she had no desire to consume any type of food. There was no way that she could go through a second round of that, but her pride wouldn't allow her to go to him, so she would wait.

She turned towards Bryan. "I'd like to be alone, if you don't mind!"

"You want me to go?" Bryan inquired.

"Please!" Myah wasn't trying to offend him, but she wanted to wallow in peace. "Can I have the spare key back that you have as well?"

Bryan stood still, he didn't know if she was ending their friendship or if she just wanted some peace and quiet, either way it was her house.

Myah noticed his hesitation. "I just don't want any interruption, that's all." She knew his feelings were hurt, but she needed some privacy. Instead of feeling sorry for herself, she planned to get even. If games were what Lance wanted, then games is what he was going to get.

When Bryan opened the door to exit, Jason stood in the doorway. Taking Bryan and Myah by surprise, Bryan quietly excused himself and Myah ushered Deja's husband inside. Until that moment, Myah didn't know that Deja's husband knew the location of her apartment. It made her a little uneasy, but she let him in nonetheless.

"Is everything alright Jason?" Myah inquired, slightly concerned.

"Have you talked to Deja?" Jason asked.

"Not since class ended!"

"How long ago was that?"

Myah was silently calculating. "Almost two weeks! What's going on?"

"Deja hasn't been home in a couple of days!" Jason confided.

"What do you mean?"

"She left a note on the nightstand when I got home three days ago and she hasn't been back since!" Jason explained.

"What did the letter say?"

"She said that she needed some time apart and once she got everything figured out, she'd be home!" Jason had started pacing the floor. "I honestly don't understand. She'll text me, but she won't answer my calls! I've been trying to be patient with her. I thought we were okay in our relationship because I honestly never saw this coming!" Jason took a deep breath. "The unknown is what's worrying me the most."

"I can only imagine!" Myah tried to sympathize. She couldn't tell Jason that Deja had probably gone off and done the ridiculous with David. One, it wasn't her place and two, she had her own problems.

To appease Jason, Myah called Deja's cell phone, but she only received the voicemail greeting. Jason ended the visit, asking Myah to call him if she heard from Deja.

Two more weeks had gone by and Myah had pulled herself together rather quickly. She had returned to work and her spirits had lifted as she prepared to show up at her parent's house for Memorial Day weekend. It was tradition for them to invite the neighborhood, barbeque and provide live entertainment. She was sure that Lance was going to be present so today would be the day that her mission would become active.

Walking towards her parent's home, she was ecstatic. The three-story; five bedroom, three bathroom, two car garage home was located in Bloomfield, Michigan. Being petty was apart of her protocol, but to be fair she reasoned that Lance started it by taking the letter and the box before she had the opportunity to seize the moment.

She clutched her arm tighter as she moved through the crowd and into the house to find her parents. Since Lance was convinced that no man wanted to be bothered with her, she vowed to prove him wrong.

Bumping into her parents, she greeted. "Mom and Dad, this is a friend of mine, Jeremiah. Jeremiah, this is Mr. & Mrs. Johnson."

Instead of her parents speaking to Myah's guest they looked at each other and replied, "You two really need to stop this." And then Michael extended his hand to Jeremiah and responded, "Please make yourself at home!"

Jeremiah was a customer that frequented Myah's family restaurant and normally Myah refuted his advances. But when he asked to take her out last week, she didn't hesitate. In fact they had been on several dates since then, convincing Myah that they had perfected the performance of a genuine couple. Maybe it was a little unethical for Myah to lead Jeremiah on, but she reasoned that there were plenty of men who had done it to women a thousand times over. The relationship was only a week old, Jeremiah would survive.

If Lance was able to leave town to check on a friend, then certainly she could entertain a friend. Myah continued the introduction's once she ran into her brother and Andréa. She was in such a good mood that she even rubbed Andréa's belly.

An hour had passed and there were no signs of Lance or Gwen and Myah was tired of being anxious. Her stomach was queasy and her nerves were completely rattled, but just as she was about to throw in the towel, they approached.

Micah must have seen them approaching at the same time as Myah because he pulled Andréa into his lap. Micah cradled her belly as her spreading frame melted into his. Myah got up and hugged Me-Ma before Lance walked her over towards the table where her parents were seated.

Once Lance returned to the small circle of family, he pounded fists with Micah, hugged Andréa and rubbed her belly. Myah waited for him to look in her direction when she smiled, but the scowl on his face replaced any words that could have fallen from his mouth.

Myah leaned into Jeremiah and whispered. "This is Lance, Micah's best-friend!"

Jeremiah nodded his head in Lance's direction. "Hey, How ya doing Boss?"

Lance didn't respond, he simply nodded his head while staring into Myah's eyes. "Let's walk and talk for a second Myah!"

"Naw, I'm good Lance, we can chill here!"

"It wasn't a question or a request, Myah!" Lance barked.

She silently stared into his eyes and something inside of her churned. She was internally conflicted; should she adhere to his command or let him cause a scene? Clearly she didn't give a shit about him being Army strong. Leaning into Jeremiah, she asked, "Give me a minute?" She arched her eyebrows as she waited for his response.

He replied with a nod.

And before Myah could rise out of her chair, Lance snatched her from the seat as he politely excused himself while tightening his hold on her arm. When they were inside the house, she snatched out of his grip. "Have you lost your mind?" She yelled at him.

"Nope, not yet." He bent down and threw her over his shoulder as he marched up the stairs to the bedroom that belonged to Myah while growing up. She kicked and screamed the entire way, but Lance ignored the beating that his back and stomach endured.

As quickly as Lance threw her on the bed, Myah got back up swinging. She was tired of his shit and lack of manners. Every time he was presented an opportunity to show his ass, he did!

Throwing her back on the bed and laying on top of her, Lance held her hostage. "Did your period come last week?"

Myah tried to knee him in the groin, but it was useless. She was pinned to the bed with very little oxygen circulating to her brain. "Lance please get off of me!"

"Answer my question!" He urged.

Myah laid there quietly, she wasn't even sure when her period was suppose to come. She normally waited for its arrival. "I don't know when it's suppose to come!" She wrapped her legs around his waist to try and get some leverage, but it was to no avail.

"It was due the eighteenth!" Lance informed.

"Of May?" Myah asked.

"Yes!"

Myah was calculating, today was May 26, 2014, the 18th was last Sunday, so she was a week late! Or, was she more than a week late because she couldn't remember the last time she had a period. *Wait, how the hell did he know when my period was due?* She asked herself.

Lance was becoming anxious. "Hello! I'm talking to you!"

"How the hell do you know when my period is due?" Myah questioned.

It was Lance's turn to become quiet.

"Hello! I'm talking to you!" Myah mocked.

"I have a period tracker for your menstrual cycle!" Lance confessed.

"YOU HAVE A WHAT?" Myah hit Lance in his side. "Get your heavy ass off of me Lance. Get off of me right now!" Before Lance could completely move off of her, Myah hit him again in the stomach. "What is wrong with you? Why are you tracking my period?"

"Would you stop yelling, Myah?"

Myah was beyond irritated. She extended her hand towards Lance while tapping her foot on the floor. "Give me your phone!"

"No!"

"Lance if you don't gi---" Before Myah could finish the sentence, Lance handed over the phone. The last thing he needed was for her to start yelling again.

Myah scrolled all the way back to March, when she first slept with him in his hotel room. Sure enough the month of May was marked for the 18th, but Myah didn't remember being sick or anything. Then the image of her throwing up in the kitchen sink and the crying spells, surfaced. She also hadn't had much of an appetite, but she thought those symptoms along with her indulgence in sleep were because she was depressed.

Myah slowly sat on the bed and Lance walked closer to her and then crouched down in between her thighs. "Me-Ma has been dreaming about fish, I know you're pregnant!"

"That's just a myth Lance!" Myah discouraged.

"Me-Ma said before you came to her last time, she had dreamed of fish."

Myah rose off the bed and handed Lance back his phone. "If you come over tomorrow, I'll take a test!"

"I have a test in the car, now!" Lance rushed.

She was flabbergasted; this man had lost his natural born mind. "What in the hell is wrong with you? I am not about to take a pregnancy test in the midst of a barbeque!"

"Then I'll come over tonight and you can take the test then!"

"Or you can come over tomorrow!"

"Myah!"

"Lance!" Myah challenged.

"Why are you trying to fight me on this?" Lance questioned.

"I'm not, it's just not the best time to have a baby!"

"And why not?"

"Because we can't even sleep in the same bed, for one!" Myah argued.

"I'll go to the PTSD group meetings!"

"You'll go to the meetings?" Myah asked skeptically!

"I love you Myah, I'll go the meetings!" Lance walked up to Myah, cradled the back of her head and pressed his lips against hers. "I Love you, I'll go to the meetings!"

Chapter 19

Myah shifted in the bed after a long night of tossing and turning to find a figure sitting in a chair across the room. Leaning on her elbow, she wiped her eyes to remove the crust that had generated in such a short time. Her initial prayer was that she was hallucinating, but low and behold, Lance had drug her dining room chair into the bedroom. He was crouched over with his elbows planted in his knees and his hands clasped together with his eyes focused on her.

"Are you trying to give me a heart attack? And how did your creepy looking ass get in here?" Myah rattled.

"I know you don't think that I'd allow Bryan to have a key and not myself!"

Myah crawled out of the bed and walked over towards Lance. "When you go to your meeting next week Honey, I want them to evaluate where you stand psychologically."

"I'm a man Myah, call it what you want!" Lance expressed his lack of concern.

Myah threw her hand up in the air to wave him off as she headed towards the bathroom.

"No wait, don't pee yet!"

"You don't pee yet Lance, I have to go to the bathroom!"

"Myah the test says that the first morning pee is the most accurate!"

"Well let me get you a paper cup from the kitchen, so you can pee in it!" She joked. "I'm probably not even pregnant; it's probably delayed because of stress."

"What stress Myah?"

"You! You're my stress and you make my ass hurt so bad, Lance! The shenanigans you pulled by leaving town to tend to *Miss Thing* plus all the other bullshit in between." She ranted.

"Myah please just go take the test!" Lance pulled three tests out of the bag. "One of these will tell us the truth!"

"Lance, I am not taking three tests!" She whined.

"Myah use the same piss for all three." He held up his hand before she could respond because she was starting to wear his patience thin. He grabbed her arm and led her to the kitchen to get a plastic cup and then into the bathroom. He furthered his assistance by pulling her pajama shirt up and pulling her underwear down.

"Lance I don't need supervision, you're making my pee afraid to come out!" Myah was still whining. She hadn't had enough sleep and Lance was frustrating her with his urgency to take this test.

"Then please just take the test Myah, damn!"

For the first time all morning, Myah noticed the strain on his face. "You want a baby, don't you?" She rubbed her hand against his cheek while staring into his glossy eyes.

"I want you Myah, I want us. So please take the test!"

Taking the boxes out of his hand, she placed them on the counter before she assumed the squatting position. Closing her eyes at the release of her bladder as she accidently filled the cup to the rim, she was relieved.

Myah went to hand Lance the cup when he stepped back. "You can't hold my cup Lance?"

"Myah would you hold my pee?" Lance counter asked.

"If you were pregnant I would!" She reasoned. "I need to wipe my ass, so please hold the cup before I pour it down the toilet and flush it. Then you'll have to wait another two hours when I have to go again." She smiled at the threat.

Lance took the cup from her hands and placed it on the bathroom sink as he tore open the seals on all three pregnancy tests. He used the Doppler in the packet as he dripped three drops per test on the spot provided.

Myah closed the lid on the toilet and sat on top of it as they waited for the results. They didn't have to wait the full two minutes that was recommended in the instructions. Within thirty seconds, all three tests displayed six lines, confirming Myah's pregnancy.

Looking at the tests and then at Lance, Myah blew out the air that she had unconsciously been holding as the tears trickled down her face. She didn't know if she was excited or scared; maybe a little of both as she recognized the same emotions flash across Lance's face.

Lance crouched down on his knees and wrapped his arms around her waist. Myah rubbed the top of his head as he kissed her stomach.

"So what now?" Myah asked Lance.

"Now you read the letter!" Lance pulled the letter out of his pocket and handed it to her.

Opening the letter, she proceeded to read every word that was printed on the page:

Kierra Smith

To know you is to love you
And it helps to cast all fear aside
To know you is to love you
And without you my world is deprived
To know you is to love you
So I'm speechless that you chose me
To know you is to love you
Because without you the wells of emptiness runs deep
To know you is to love you
So, I know where I belong
To know you is to love you
Please trust that I'll come back home

P.S. nothing or no one could ever take your place. You're everything that I'll ever want and you fill every void that was once a need.
I love you Myah Michelle Johnson

Lance watched the look of astonishment spread across Myah's face as he positioned his body to leave one knee on the ground. He pulled the box from his pocket and said:

"I was wrong for leaving you six years ago. I can't make- up for the past, but I have the power to alter the present and change the future. If you'll allow me to; I'd love to be your friend, your lover, your provider, your husband and a father to our unborn child. Myah Michelle Johnson, Will You Marry Me?"

The tears that formed while reading the poem had turned into a full blown sob. Myah couldn't get the answer passed her throat so she nodded her head up and down to say "Yes". Lance was everything that she ever wanted and everything that she needed. In that moment, she vowed that she would find a way to ensure that every area of his life was filled with love and support.

She'd be there to comfort every fear and uplift every dream and goal because she was there for the long-haul. Lance had been her first, but he was certain that he wanted her to be his last. Regardless of the past and uncertain of the future, they were destined to be - because without him, she was doomed!

Epilogue

Deja nervously walked into the Doubletree hotel in downtown, Detroit. She had gone against every ethic and moral code of conduct that she believed in, but she needed answers and she wanted them today!

Stopping at the front desk, Deja retrieved the key that David had left for her. She listened to the clerk confirm the room number that David had texted and then made her way to the elevator. Her mind was racing as she approached the door; David was hiding from his fiancé and she was hiding from her husband.

Hopefully they would be able to figure this out and return back to their lives, immediately. Sliding the key into the slot and turning the handle, Deja entered the room.

The suite was breath-taking with an elegance captured only in a home decorating magazine. The living room housed: a sofa, chair, desk, flat screen TV with a small microwave and refrigerator to match.

David sat on the left side of the sofa, closer to the wall and with a small nod Deja walked passed him. She couldn't help feel the warmth that exuding from the interior, leaving the impression of a home. The ceramic marble in the bathroom and the large king size bed was alluring, to say the least.

She took off her shoes and sat on the couch with David, tucking her feet under her butt, she made herself comfortable.

David silently admired how beautiful she was. She had been apart of his life for as long as he could remember. He couldn't pin-point when he had stopped seeing her as a girl and more along the lines of a woman, but he had. "So what's up Big Head?"

"You tell me!" Deja smirked.

"You said that you wanted answers, I want to give them to you!" David explained.

"If you could have traded her virginity for mine, would you?" Deja asked abruptly.

"Whose?"

"Your fiancé's!"

David took a long, hard look at her before replying, "Yes!"

"Why?" She urged. His one word response wasn't sufficient.

"You and I have history and that alone makes the circumstances different. Your husband doesn't fit into the family like I do and neither does she!"

"It's because you've been around longer and because your brother's been married to my sister for the last ten years. Not to mention that they dated five years prior to that!"

"Do you honestly believe that's the only reason?"

"You left David."

"You pushed me away. Did you expect me to stay and fight for you?"

"I pushed you away because it wouldn't have worked!"

"And why not?" David demanded an answer; he wanted closure just like she did.

"Because I was afraid of the history. I couldn't give you my virginity because I didn't know how!"

David remained silent because he was puzzled.

Deja continued to clarify her last statement. "With your reputation, I knew that eventually you'd want to take the relationship to the next level and I'd have to perform on a certain level to keep you! I didn't know how!"

"You don't think that I would have understood that? If you had talked to me, then I could have told you that I only wanted you, I only needed you!" David regretfully explained.

"I couldn't... I didn't know how to tell you without being embarrassed. I figured that it was better to be safe than sorry, so I sabotaged it."

"Unfortunately Big Head, that's a sorry ass excuse!" David wasn't cutting Deja any slack because he had sat up thinking many nights. He had lusted and longed for her and it had taken him years to come to terms with fact that she wasn't coming back.

"What about you? You didn't fight for us either and that makes you just as guilty." She blamed.

"I came to you before you married Jason!" David yelled.

"It was the week of my wedding. What was I suppose to do?"

"You were supposed to follow your heart!" He reasoned.

"Like how you're following your heart by marrying her?"

"I love her!"

"Do you? Then why are you here with me?" Deja questioned.

"The same reason you're here with me!" He retorted.

Deja was silent. "I just wanna make peace with this. I wanna be okay with the fact that you're getting married."

"I can't help you deal with that. That's something you'll have to come to terms with on your own!"

Deja was wounded, this was a hard pill to swallow and she hadn't been prepared for it! "So what now?" She whispered.

"There's nothing to do. I've waited on you long enough, don't you think?" David turned towards the bedroom and Deja followed his gaze!

"Oh yeah, the fuck or fight proposition, right?"

"I mean, I feel like it's the only thing left to do!" David rationalized.

Something inside Deja clicked and confirmation set in on why she hadn't looked back once she left David. He had some more maturing to do and she hoped that his fiancé could assist. She walked up to David and kissed him on the cheek before whispering, "One day you'll comprehend that sex doesn't equate to love and fortunately for me, I understand that sex can't fix what's broken between us."

Deja put on her shoes and walked towards the door. "I wish you guys the best in your upcoming nuptials because this relationship…" She pointed at David and then at herself. "Is officially doomed."

Without another word, she exited the room and strolled towards the elevator. Deja had made a final decision and she was ready to go home!

Turn The Page To See What's Coming Next!

Good Girls With Bad Girl Tendency's (Chrissey Williams)

Chapter 1

The way that indecision hung in the air, one would have thought that Chrissey was staring down the barrel of a gun. But, it was much simpler than that as she watched her male companion check into the Westin Hotel with his side-piece.

Chrissey's first thought was to just set the car on fire with the emergency gasoline that she kept in her truck. And if she had to place a bet on this situation, she would deem it as a crisis. For the first time in her life, she was at a cross-road and she needed a little assistance. She backed in between the bushes near the entrance, pulling her cell phone out of her pocket and dialed the sister that was closest to her location.

When the connection broke in the line, Chrissey heard the sleep lingering in Carla's voice. "Hello?" When Carla didn't get a response, she repeated herself. "Hello?"

"Oh sorry Carla, I got distracted." Chrissey answered.

Carla breathed a sigh of relief. "What's going on Pooty?"

Chrissey paused. "I think we should set his car on fire!"

Lifting her body out of the bed, Carla needed to ensure that she heard Chrissey correctly. "Who? Set whose car on fire?"

"Daniel's car!" Chrissey whispered.

"Oh My God, where are you?" Carla had gotten out of bed and began moving around to find some clothes that she could actually fit.

"At the Westin Hotel, right here on Ten Mile right passed Evergreen." She informed.

"Okay Chrissey, well wait a damn minute, let me call Morgan and Ebony!"

"Ugh, are you trying to incriminate all of us?" Chrissey asked.

"Dude, I'm not going to jail by myself! Are you trying to send me into premature labor?" Carla was an octave just above yelling.

"Okay, Okay, Okay, just hurry up. I can't keep hiding in these bushes!" Chrissey said as she disconnected the call.

Carla looked at the phone as the line went dead. "Bushes? This girl has completely gone off the deep end!" Tapping the phone icon on her Note 3, she called Morgan and then Ebony as she slipped on her shoes and grabbed her jacket.

Ten minutes later, Chrissey watched as Carla's Jeep pulled into the parking lot, followed by Ebony's and then Morgan's. Chrissey figured it was safe to come out of hiding when her phone chimed and Carla asked the location of the bush that she hid under.

Chrissey stepped out front and sprinted towards her sisters and Morgan, which was more like a sister, but Carla's best-friend.

"Where is your car?" Ebony questioned.

"I switched cars with Tasha. Hello, I couldn't do a following detail in my own automobile." Chrissey informed.

"So what the hell is going on?" Morgan butted in.

"Daniel and his troll just went into the hotel. And I think we should set his car on fire!"

"Woah, Arson is not going to look good on my record. You know I just got that one thing cleared." Ebony admitted.

"Can we just paint the car a different color? I mean its white, so we can paint it any color!" Carla suggested.

"Or we could puncture every tire and leave a few eggs on the windshield!" Morgan countered.

"I like that!" Carla agreed with Morgan. "But only puncture three tires."

"Why only three tires?" Morgan asked.

"Because the insurance company will pay for it to be fixed if all four tires are flat. But if we only do three, then he's screwed." Carla explained.

"Listen, I want to torch his shit! I want his cheating ass to walk home!" Chrissey was fuming.

"Whatever we do, we can't keep standing here. I'm sure there is a camera somewhere watching while we stand here plotting." Carla announced.

"Well the way your stomach has expanded, hiding you is not an option at this point and time." Morgan rubbed Carla's protruding stomach.

"I see your bald- headed ass got jokes. Its 2am and you got fat people jokes." Carla moved her stomach out of Morgan's reach.

"Aww come here big girl, don't be offended. Pregnancy agrees with you, you had six months of just hips and booty and now you have a little bit of belly." Morgan tried to hug Carla.

"Can y'all two fruit cakes stay focused?" Chrissey raised her hand in the air to get their attention.

"I'll take a Vandalism charge over Arson." Ebony interjected.

"Ok, I have a can of red paint in the car!" Chrissey obliged.

"So you're a carpenter now?" Ebony asked jokingly.

Chrissey's only reply was a smirk. No one knew that she had been planning this heist for weeks. Daniel wasn't her boyfriend per se, but she didn't believe in community dick because she didn't walk around making public announcements about free coochie.

While they worked effectively and efficiently, Morgan extracted her pocket knife in and out of the three tires. Ebony teepee'd the car with tissue and napkins from her glove compartment that stuck nicely to the egg yolk that Carla's hungry ass provided.

Of course Chrissey wasn't going to be out-done by her creative sisters. She painted the word **'Dirty'** on the right side of the car and the word **'Dick'** on the left side. Once they were satisfied with their handiwork, all four girls slipped behind the wheels of their vehicles with an agreement to meet for lunch once everyone got some sleep.

Chapter 2

All the girls slid into the booth at Bar 7 in Southfield, which had become their safe haven. They talked about their problems, fears and their men at this location. When the sisters called a meeting, nothing was off-limits for discussion.

Chrissey was the last one to sit at the table because she was late as usual. "Did you guys order yet? I'm starving!"

"I ordered chicken wings!" Carla spoke first.

"I ordered spinach dip." Ebony countered.

"And I ordered the hamburger sliders." Morgan confirmed.

"Good, I'll get the cajun chicken and shrimp pasta." Chrissey settled.

"So, Chrissey could you be so kind to explain to us, why in the hell we did that to that man's Challenger? When in fact, you don't have a commitment with him nor do you want one!" Carla sparked the conversation.

"Carla it's the principle! Would you allow Joshua to go off and be with another woman, without consequences?" Chrissey confronted.

"Uh lil crazy? I'm having his baby and we are cohabitating. He can't go to the bathroom without me getting suspicious. There is no way that he would make it to a hotel room without me body bagging his ass first."

"Exactly!" Chrissey agreed.

"But, Chrissey you said out of your own mouth that you don't do relationships or commitments. So why be so crazy?" Morgan asked.

"Because I like him!" Chrissey exclaimed.

"Don't tell me we just did all that shit because she "*likes*" him!" Ebony's irritation was growing.

"This clown just made us her puppets!" Morgan laughed.

"How long have you been messing with Daniel, Chrissey?" Carla was trying to calculate.

"Off and on for two years!" Chrissey admitted.

"Okay well until your twenty-six year old ass grows up enough to admit that you have deeper feelings for him, don't call my pregnant ass any more, unless it's a damn emergency." Carla scolded.

"Agreed." Morgan chimed.

"Agreed." Ebony reaffirmed.

"Fine!" Chrissey mumbled.

"And just so we're clear," Carla added. "Emergencies are incidents that involve blood, tragedies that are death related and crimes that accompany jail time!"

Everyone laughed at Carla's inability to be subtle with her explanation.

For the remainder of the meal, casual conversation floated over and around Chrissey, but she wasn't paying attention to any of it. She was reflecting on what her sisters had said and although it stung a bit, Chrissey could respect it as the truth.

Maybe Daniel felt that he hadn't owed her anything because of the label or the lack thereof on their relationship. But, it was in Chrissey's experience that you couldn't trust street men because the only woman that governed their hearts, were the Almighty Dollar.

She had been in the game so long that she understood that a man loved his money more than his woman and if he cared about her then he spent his money on her. And maybe that was why the hotel scene had gotten to her so badly. If Daniel was willing to treat the side-piece to the Westin then that meant she wasn't a Motel 6 kind of tramp.

Chrissey had fallen in love with money at the age of sixteen; she wasn't sure where the fascination had come from. But the desire for wanting to look good had surfaced right around the time that her breast had blossomed from a bird's chest to a bird's nest.

Her sisters were content with having clothes that looked cute, but she wouldn't settle until every pair of jeans and every shirt that she owned was labeled with a name-brand logo on it. Chrissey understood what men wanted from women. So instead of being a doormat or a storage bucket for a man's cum, she observed and acquired the technique to play the game.

Men wanted sex and she wanted security, which ultimately equaled money. The way she figured it, she hadn't strayed too far from God because the bible even acknowledged that money answered all things. And since the men were calling, she didn't mind answering as long as money was on the other end of it.

Now that didn't make her money hungry and it for damn sure didn't make her Hoe. Chrissey understood that you could get what you wanted from a man without ever spreading your legs. Her mother Eileen had continuously stressed how valuable your vagina was and the price that it held. Eileen would say, "THIS IS GOLD, IF A MAN LOVES YOU, HE WILL MARRY YOU TO UNCOVER THE TREASURE."

Chrissey agreed with her mother's logic to a certain extent, but her bills weren't going to pay themselves based on gold and treasure. She had been with Daniel out of convenience initially, but if she were honest with herself, she cared more than she led on. Unfortunately, voicing those feelings would cost her more than she was willing to risk.

Paying the bill and departing from her sister's approximately two hours later, Chrissey figured that she might as well stop by Daniel's house and check on him. She couldn't help laugh to herself. *What had his face looked like when he checked out of the hotel this morning?* Chrissey was sure that he was embarrassed and possibly humiliated, but he would think that next time he wanted to step out.

Pulling into the driveway of Daniel's condo off of Northwestern Highway, Chrissey put the car in park behind the vandalized Challenger muscle car. She exhaled as she was gearing herself for the fight of her life. She demanded respect and if she had to tear up all of his shit until she got it then that's exactly what she was prepared to do.

Instead of using her key, Chrissey decided that it was best to knock first. She wasn't willing to walk into the house blind-sided.

Everything was so quiet that her feet automatically began scuffling because her nerves were on edge. Chrissey saw the car and assumed that Daniel was in the house, but she didn't hear his body shuffling to get to the door. Just as she was about to insert her key in the door knob, it turned and slowly screeched open.

Chrissey looked at the figure that hid in the shadows as she noticed that his 9 mm hung loosely in his left hand. Not sure if she should run or scream, she slowly began backing away from the door, when he called out. "Hell naw, you better get your ass in this house Chrissey."

With her hands in a surrendering stance Chrissey replied, "You know Babe, I don't think today is a good day! Maybe I'll come back tomorrow."

This time when Daniel spoke to her, he used the gun as his hand movements, escorting her into the house. "Chrissey I'm not playing with your bi-polar, crazy, dysfunctional, psycho ass. Now would be the time for you to get your ass in this house."

Gaining boldness from the adjectives that dripped with disdain as Daniel used them to describe her mental capacity, Chrissey walked under the threshold. "And ain't nobody playing with your cheating, retarded, wining and dining, hotel spending, late night creeping, you wish your chick was dumb, having ass."

Without saying another word, Daniel, who stood a foot over Chrissey's frame, backed her into the living room as he sat on the sofa. He wondered to himself why he continued to deal with her dramatized actions, when there were plenty of women who were willing to commit to him. Lifting his head he asked, "Can you please tell me why you are so irrational?"

"What do you mean?" Chrissey asked somewhat confused.

"Why in the hell would you do that to my car Chrissey Rochelle Williams? What on God's green-earth possessed you to redecorate my damn car?"

"What in God's green-earth would possess you to cheat on me?" She retorted.

"In order for me to cheat on you, it would deem that we are in a relationship, which you clarified was not the case!"

"So do you think that gave you walking papers to do whatever you wanted?" Chrissey questioned.

"Why not, you seem to!" Daniel spat.

"Well then that's why your car looks like that! You've gots to be more careful!" Chrissey threw her hands up in the air.

Rising to his feet, Daniel walked back to his door. "Chrissey get out of my house, before I beat you like a nicca in the streets!"

Gathering her purse over her shoulder, she pranced towards the door. "Gladly!" When she got back over the threshold, she looked over her shoulder and stuck her tongue out at him! *I am such a stinker,* she thought to herself.

Behind the wheel of her car, Chrissey began thinking about that morning's events. She wasn't too worried about Daniel, he would calm down eventually. But, what had her life come to? She didn't want to commit because she wasn't alone, but she was lonely. The only thrills that excited her were the unacceptable and hazardously insane dummy missions that she and her sisters created and conquered.

Before Chrissey knew it, the blue and red lights reflected in her rear-view mirror and for a brief second, she contemplated out-driving the police in the S550 Mercedes Benz. All kinds of thoughts attacked her. What if Daniel had sent the police after her on a charge for Vandalism and destruction of property? But then again, he wouldn't do that because it would draw too much attention to himself and his line of work.

Pulling over and putting the car in park, Chrissey rested her head on the headrest. She slowly rolled down her window to await the officer who was walking in her direction.

When the officer arrived at the driver door, Chrissey hadn't expected him to look so dreamy. "Officer?"

"Ma'am do you know why I pulled you over?" The Officer responded.

"No Sir, I do not!" Chrissey smiled.

"You were going ten miles over the speed-limit in this residential area. License and Registration, please." He recited.

"Actually, I don't have my license on me, but I can give you any information that you need."

"You don't have your Driver's License?" The Officer asked warily.

"No sir, I do not."

"Do you have an active Driver's License?" The Officer questioned.

"Yes, if you want to run my information through the system, My name is Carla Camille Williams and I live on Winchester in Southfield, Mi." Chrissey stated.

"Carla huh?" The officer eyed her suspiciously. "You know normally when a driver rattles off their information like that, it usually belongs to a relative or sibling."

"Well I'm sorry that you've had to entertain such foolery before now. But, if you would like to run my information then you'll find the truth."

"I'm sure I will Carla. Give me your number!" The officer requested while pulling the pad out of his back pocket.

Chrissey gave her real telephone number and Carla's home information. The officer let her off with a warning and advised that he would be in touch. Chrissey needed a game plan and some finality in her life. So her new goal was to create an exit strategy from the tainted and deceitful environment that she had become prisoner to. Putting her car into drive, she pulled off of the curb and headed towards destiny.

The Counterfeit
Sequel To: CCW & The Game Changer

L ying across the bed, Joshua was exhausted. He and Carla had gone through the motions of figuring out who would have to compromise on their relocation. If he moved to Michigan there would be no room for him inside of Serenity Bank and if she moved to Chicago, her fate held unemployment as well. Of course there was the half of million dollars that was still in Joshua's possession. But, it was now considered blood-money because men like Dre, were looking for a money trail. Joshua was too street-smart to give Dre the satisfaction of falling into his trap.

The more Joshua thought about it, the more inconvenient this dilemma was becoming. Every time he turned around Carla was: crying, whining, yelling, sleeping, eating, peeing or just plain ole horny. She had more mood swings and indecisive moments than a toddler battling the terrible two syndrome.

Oh and there was no way that he could forget how Carla constantly hogged the bathtub because she complained of how the steam from the shower tampered with her curls!

"This shit is played out!" Joshua whispered under his breath. His youngest child was twenty-one, how in the hell did he expect to start over with a newborn? The wages of sex had to be death or pregnancy because right about now, the two seemed to be one in the same.

The closer Carla's due date came, the more anxious Joshua grew and his patience waivered. He was begging that there was a light at the end of the tunnel. It wasn't as if he didn't love Carla. God he loved her; the way she smelled and the taste that she left lingering on his tongue was intoxicating. He had even grown to love her family as his own, but this pregnancy was starting to wear on his nerves.

Joshua had Dre on his ass, Vanessa in his ear and a dead baby that constantly invaded his dreams. If he never needed some direction before, now was the time. Joshua could sense danger a mile away and his sixth sense told him that it wasn't far from his reach. He had to get Carla and the baby out of sight and soon because time was definitely not on his side.